Olivia Rupprecht
Hurts So Good

BANTAM BOOKS

NEW YORK · TORONTO · LONDON · SYDNEY · AUCKLAND

HURTS SO GOOD

A Bantam Book / November 1992

If you would be interested in receiving protective vinyl
covers for your Loveswept books, please write to this address
for information:

Loveswept
Bantam Books
P.O. Box 985
Hicksville, NY 11802

ISBN 0-553-44308-9

Published simultaneously in the United States and Canada

Bantam Books are published by Bantam Books, a division of
Bantam Doubleday Dell Publishing Group, Inc. Its trademark,
consisting of the words "Bantam Books" and the portrayal of
a rooster, is Registered in U.S. Patent and Trademark Office
and in other countries. Marca Registrada. Bantam Books, 666
Fifth Avenue, New York, New York 10103.

PRINTED IN THE UNITED STATES OF AMERICA

OPM   0 9 8 7 6 5 4 3 2 1

"Go home, *chère*," Neil pleaded.

Andrea felt his arms tighten around her as he spoke.

"You're courtin' trouble if you stay here," he warned her. "I'm the trouble, and you won't be safe in the same city. I feel something for you and that's risky—for both of us." He handed her several folded bills. "Take this and buy a ticket on the next plane to somewhere else. Don't come back. Keep your distance and keep it good."

Andrea felt torn apart inside. Her body still tingled where he'd touched her; and where his lips had brushed, she felt she'd been kissed by an angel. He claimed to be the devil's own and yet he sought to protect her from himself. She'd tasted forbidden, thrilling excitement . . . a dangerous rush. "Keep your money, Slick," she said quietly. "I'm not keeping my distance. . . ."

WHAT ARE *LOVESWEPT* ROMANCES?

They are stories of true romance and touching emotion. We believe those two very important ingredients are constants in our highly sensual and very believable stories in the *LOVESWEPT* line. Our goal is to give you, the reader, stories of consistently high quality that may sometimes make you laugh, sometimes make you cry, but are always fresh and creative and contain many delightful surprises within their pages.

Most romance fans read an enormous number of books. Those they truly love, they keep. Others may be traded with friends and soon forgotten. We hope that each *LOVESWEPT* romance will be a treasure—a "keeper." We will always try to publish

LOVE STORIES YOU'LL NEVER FORGET
BY AUTHORS YOU'LL ALWAYS REMEMBER

The Editors

*Special thanks go to Mr. Homer Brown,
professional saxophonist and a
gentleman, first class.
Sayonara Binbo, Homer—
From one of the Six Pack at El Chapultepec*

Author's Note

"Where do you get your ideas?" is a question often asked of a writer, and the answer is an elusive one. A picture, song or dream, a personal experience, an overheard conversation between strangers—all make fine fodder for the imagination.

And yet, no matter how riveting or original the plot, the hallmark of memorable stories is the strength of compelling characters. To deny them the right to speak for themselves is to be guilty of author intrusion.

Why am I telling you this? Because you're about to meet some special people who speak a dialect that is vibrant, unique, rich. Forget the Queen's English. We's in N'awlins, y'all. A city that's divinely decadent, a world set apart by its zest for life and colorful inhabitants.

Lou and Liza, and to a lesser extent Neil, are part of a community I bow to in honor of its societal contributions. So please do not construe my effort at portrayal of these characters as an exercise in prejudice when it is my wish to salute the various cultures that give our country dimension.

One

There was a gentle cruelty about his mouth. Perhaps it was in the hard yet pliable fullness of his lips. Or the way they sensuously parted for his tongue to stroke them and leave a light sheen of moisture before curling into a sneer.

His mouth descended, then paused before claiming the instrument of his desire. At first touch Andrea's own mouth quivered in response, then the low croon of a saxophone seduced her ears.

The clink of ice to glass was Neil Grey's only accompaniment in the smoky bar—that, and the quick scratch of pen to paper. As Andrea Post glanced up from her table at the front, she stopped in mid-scribble.

Neil's hazel eyes connected with hers. He raised a single brow in acknowledgment, then dismissed her presence as he went about making love to the saxophone with his trademark pucker and blow.

Once again she succumbed to the spell he wove in a performance as uniquely his as his coveted compositions. The smooth swivel of his hips eased into a sexy gyration, and then, in a show of his mastery of the stage, he hoofed, crouched, lunged, and waltzed. He was an outrageous flirt, a naughty lover and a

James Dean tough who pouted and winked, then stroked his sax between his legs while tossing out a "Beat it or eat it" grin.

The rest of the band was now backing him up, but Andrea tuned them out, second fiddles all to this man's stunning gift. She put down her pen, sensing that she, and the rapt audience who swayed to his beat from the edge of their chairs, were being humored by a condescending artist. A master musician who allowed them to listen as long as they respected his intimate dialogue with his instrument, didn't cramp his style, and paid the bills.

Without exception, all acquiesced. Neil Grey, with a past as infamous as it was famous, was hot, even hotter than when he'd reached the top before hitting rock bottom.

"My, what a colorful background you have, Ms. Post. At the ripe old age of twenty-five you have a helluva track record in the odd-job department, but no experience tending bar." A few minutes after the last set of the night, Neil was in his office at the back of the bar, tapping the application on the big old desk he felt a kinship with. Nicked up, shoved around, but obstinately standing despite the wear and tear. "Lookin' to expand your résumé to include making cocktails, garnishes, and dealing with drunks?"

"I'm a fast learner, Mr. Grey. And I want the job." When he continued to scrutinize her application, she added quickly, "I'll even work the first week for free. If you're not completely satisfied with my services, you can tell me to leave. You have everything to gain and nothing to lose by taking a chance on me."

She looked as sincere as she sounded. Sure, sister, he thought, where'd you come from, some off-off Broadway show? No one gave away something for nothing, and those services she was talking about likely had some strings attached.

"That a fact?" he drawled. Neil laced his fingers behind his head and pursed the lips he'd noticed her staring at throughout the performance. Hers were so soft and full that he just might offer to pay her for a few hours of heavy smooching once he got to the bottom of her game. Kissing matches, one of his favorite exercises.

"Tell me, *chère,* you really here for the open position behind my bar, or did you have some other 'open position' in mind? Maybe we can strike a deal on one if not the other."

She sat straighter in her chair, and the cat-green eyes that had been focused on his mouth snapped up to his.

"I beg your pardon?" Her face turned a lively shade. But he couldn't tell if this "pet groomer, pizza maker, disk jockey" was excited or shocked. Either way, she was a dish, and he liked listening to her clean, supple voice.

"Are you a groupie?"

"A groupie!" Her jaw dropped, revealing slightly spaced front teeth. Maybe she wasn't a groupie. Maybe she was one of those nice gals Lou always said were around somewhere. Only the way Neil figured it, they were after something too. Stuff like respect and commitment and saving his unsavable soul.

"A groupie," she repeated, pinning him with a glare. "What ever gave you *that* idea?"

"The way you've been looking at me. It's . . . familiar." Her blush was becoming. Kind of cute. And such a rare sight, he wanted her to do it some more before he tossed her out. "And I seen—*saw* you in the audience several times this week. You left the same way you came—alone—so I take it you aren't a hooker prowling the French Quarter for a trick."

"Absolutely not," she gasped. "And since when was it a crime to enjoy one's own company?"

"Not a crime, but a foxy woman doing the local hot spots by herself and dressed to kill—by the way, that snappy purple jumpsuit is just your color, *chère*—struck me as peculiar."

She suddenly stood, gripped the edge of his desk, and stared down at him with an icy look that could've put out a New Orleans heat wave. She was something to behold, with red hair, red lips, and even redder cheeks. Flame. His favorite color. Damn.

"Mr. Grey, let's get this straight. Just because I'm a fan who admittedly owns every record you've ever cut, and just because one reason I'd like to work here is so I can get in without paying your hefty cover charge, that doesn't mean I would ever consider it a privilege to sleep with a stranger who obviously has an ego to match his outrageous presumptions."

Neil mentally added "spitfire mama with a Webster" to her résumé. Squelching laughter, he motioned her back to her seat and faked a chagrined expression.

"Sorry if I jumped to the wrong conclusion, but I had to make sure. Shades of Grey ain't no dive—" Damn, he'd slipped again, sounding like the poor boy he'd been before learning the proper talk that went with his highfalutin station in life. "What I mean is, this is a respectable establishment, and I have every intention of keeping it that way. This place is more than a nightclub to me. It's . . ."

He paused. Why was he trying to explain himself, and why was she no longer piqued but leaning forward as if hungry for a tidbit of juicy gossip? Hadn't he learned to keep his mouth shut and *never* to trust a woman with a confidence? Whether it was a free ticket to a concert or a free lunch, otherwise known as alimony, these gold diggers always wanted something, always looked out for number one. *Women.* Didn't trust them farther than he could spit.

Neil slipped a well-worn flask from his back pocket and took a swallow.

"It's tasty," he pronounced. "Better than a bad woman on a good day." Smacking his lips, he waited for her to sniff in disgust and slam out of the office.

"I'm sure that's an educated assessment," she said in a bored voice. "Getting back to your opening for a bartender . . ."

While she got down to business, he got down to the fact that she looked like a woman who fixed her hair so a man could mess it up, a woman who kissed back as good as she got. Just the kind a man could take home to Mama, then make it with in the backseat. Sure would be fun to find out if she was for sure.

All the more reason to get her out of there before he could do something stupid and give her the job. But he couldn't toss her out on her shapely butt because he was attracted, *real* attracted, so Neil decided to give her an incentive to scram.

"And furthermore, Mr. Grey—"

"Like to play darts?" he cut in.

"Darts? They're all right, I guess, but I'm better at pool. Why? Are you setting up a game area in the bar?"

"The game's here, *chère*," he said, tapping his desk with a finger. "Meanest game in town, and I'm the reigning champ. Care for a demo?" Neil pulled the rubber band off his short ponytail. Taking aim, he let the elastic fly.

Andrea jumped as the rubber band whizzed past her ear.

"Bull's-eye," he whispered with a satisfied smirk as he looked at his target.

She glanced over her shoulder.

The rubber band hung from a dart that was stuck in the cleavage of a life-size pinup displayed between glossies of Dizzy Gillespie and Al Hirt. The dart in question was one of many decorating various body parts of a glamorous woman Andrea recognized as his ex-wife.

Andrea cleared her throat and took a deep breath. "Good shot," she said, managing a smile.

"Lots of practice." He cut his eyes back to hers, and she commanded herself to ignore the sweat beading her brow. When she didn't comment, he dug into the top desk drawer and profered a dart. "Double or nothing says you can't zap the navel."

"I'd rather finish the interview, if you don't mind."

"I mind. Take the dart," he ordered. "Zap the navel, get the job. Miss, and you're out of here. It's how I hire all of my people. Proprietor's prerogative."

He was actually serious! If there was a fine line between genius and madness, he had to be straddling that line. Was this man capable of smashing cameras and smacking his fist into reporters' faces? She didn't doubt that and more.

But that and more had all been covered by the tabloids with glee. Andrea didn't want to copy other journalists and dig around Neil's ample dirt. As a professional, she had to find a new angle.

As a woman, she already found him unnerving. She was careful to maintain her distance with most men, but even with the desk between them, Neil invaded her body space.

"The dart? Or the door?" His gaze lingered on her bosom. She felt uncomfortably warm from his visual caress, which seemed more intimate than any she'd ever dealt with. When she crossed her arms, he slid his gaze to her face. And winked!

Her palms sweaty, she grabbed the dart he twirled.

"Good choice," he said with approval. "Never did like quitters. You may now take four steps forward. Not big ones, mind you, 'cause that's cheating, and I never could stand cheats any more than quitters."

What was riding on her performance caused her knees to knock and her hand to shake while she took four paces forward. If she didn't zap a navel, it would be good-bye to a *Rolling Stone* byline. She'd be singing the blues as just another unsyndicated columnist who racked up the occasional magazine sale. Decent credentials, but nothing spectacular. Of course, considering the job she'd done on her application, she could try her hand at fiction.

"Is this okay?" she asked, her body tensing as anxiety pressed in and the cause of it moved nearer.

"Just right." His voice was raspy, like worn sandpaper polishing raw wood. Her stomach lurched when he stopped scant inches behind her. His breath skimmed the top of her head, and her scalp prickled. He was so close, she could smell him.

The clean scent of his cologne mingled with the muskiness of cooled sweat and a whiff of brandy. His fondness for booze, she'd learned in the course of the excruciating interview, wasn't just rumor. And neither was his hostility toward his ex-wife. Now that Andrea was only ten feet away from the poster and could see the pin-sized holes all over it, she decided the couple's public brawls hadn't been sensationalized spats after all.

"Ready . . ."

His fingers circled her wrist. She felt an uneasy lick of awareness as he drew her arm back and their elbows touched. Andrea stiffened. His short laugh wasn't a pleasant sound.

"Aim . . ."

Dear Lord, was she actually so desperate to prove she was a winner that she would willingly humor this man and delve into his obviously unstable psyche? She was.

"Fire!"

The dart sailed from her grip, and she silently pleaded for it to hit the navel. As if in slow motion she watched the point dip, then stab the ex-Mrs. Grey's crotch.

"Damn," Andrea groaned. "Let me have another try. Please? I'll get her navel if it's the last thing I do."

Even if it took her all night and then some, she would. Giving up wasn't an option, never had been—and especially not now.

She turned, expecting anything but his snicker as he continued to stare at the dart.

"Good sports who aren't quitters or cheats get extra points." He was slow to release his hold on her wrist, but once he did, he scowled at his fingertips. And then at her.

"I call the shots, and you pour them, okay?" he said.

"Then I get the job?"

"Minimum-wage-and-a-half plus tips—*if* you're as fast a learner as you say you are. Generous man that I am, I'll give you a week—with pay—to prove you're worth the risk."

Tempted as she was to take his offer and make a quick exit, Andrea seized the opportunity to explore his reasoning.

"Since I have no experience, and I did miss, I can't help but wonder why? You're known for a lot of things, Mr. Grey, but generosity isn't one of them."

"No one knows me, and especially not you," he said flatly. When she met his squint with a level stare, he fished a cigarette from his pocket along with a matchbook. He hitched a heel, struck a match against it, and lit the cigarette dangling from his lips.

She held her breath as he took several drags, then studied the rings he set afloat. With his strangely haunted eyes focused on something other than her, she shifted her attention to his hawklike face, which sported a two-day growth of salt-and-pepper beard. It matched the hair that was too long for her liking but somehow suited him. Brushed straight back from his prominent forehead, it fell straight to his chin and framed slightly hollow cheeks. He didn't look thirty-four. His reputation for hard living was etched into crow's-feet and a creased brow.

He was a tall man. Big-boned, she thought, but

couldn't be sure with his black baggy trousers and red suspenders strapped over an oversized crisp white shirt.

"I still don't understand why you're willing to hire me," she persisted, despite her urge to escape. Was lunacy contagious? she wondered. Could be, because she'd have to be as crazy as he to be drawn to the animal magnetism he wore like a pair of throwaway jeans.

He took a lazy drag, and she half expected him to blow the smoke into her face. But he blew it through his nostrils, reminding her of a fire-breathing dragon. A very sexy dragon, one a woman might take to bed but never home to her parents.

She claimed a forfeit on both options.

"Why? It's like this, Andrea—and that's Neil to you, now that you're on the payroll—you're hired because you're nice to look at and assertive without being bitchy. Qualities I put more store in than the ability to slosh hard stuff into a glass and top it off with a cherry. Cherries, *yum*, my favorite fruit. Red. Delicious. Succulent and sweet, until you bite into the pit and break a tooth." He snapped his teeth together twice, revealing a chipped front tooth.

"Any more questions?" He rolled the cigarette between well-manicured fingers.

"When do I start?"

"Be here tomorrow at five. Sharp. Even good sports get their lunch eaten by me when they're late. And I do prefer to dig in rather than mind my manners."

"Yes, Mr. Grey," she said, avoiding the use of his first name, "I can imagine that you do." She was rewarded with his perplexed frown, and then his equally perplexing bark of laughter.

"You're a tough little number, ain't you, *chère*? Guess I'd better nibble carefully on you. Be smart and skedaddle before I decide to take back the job and offer you the privilege of sleeping with a stranger who, ah"—he flicked his ashes onto the worn carpet and grinned wolfishly—"oh yes, has an ego to match his outrageous presumptions."

Andrea took the hint, as well as the job, and hurriedly left the office. As she rested her head against the door, she heard the distinct sound of a dart sinking into wood.

She left with more than a job and bright prospects ahead. She left with the knowledge that Neil Grey, despite his success and stranger than strange quirks, was not a happy man.

Two

By 3:00 A.M. the following morning, Andrea braced herself for the possibility that her employer was going to be not only unhappy, but furious. The bartender who was to train her had called in sick.

With the last chair turned up, the hardwood floor swept clean, and every waitress gone, Andrea surveyed the aftermath of a nightmare. Glasses were scattered from one end to the other of the long mahogany bar. Ashtrays brimmed with crushed-out butts. Behind her, bottles were in disarray: scotch, beer, wine, vodka, and liqueurs she'd never even heard of before they'd been ordered. On the floor lay puddles of spilled drinks.

"Buy you a drink?" asked Lou, the pianist and last musician to leave. "Looks like you could use one, chile."

"Thanks, Lou, but if I never see another highball again, it'll be too soon." She summoned a weary smile as he leaned against the bar. His chocolate eyes crinkling at the corners, he smiled with the innate kindness she'd sensed in him when he'd welcomed her aboard. She could use some kindness. Her back hurt. Her feet hurt. Even her skin hurt.

But what hurt most was feeling like a failure.

"Now, chile, don't you fret, 'cause Big Daddy's here to help. I'll get dis, you get dat, an' 'fore you know it, we'll have the place shinier than a new penny."

Andrea suppressed the urge to throw her arms around his neck in thanks. She'd never had a daddy, much less a Big Daddy who was as cuddly as her frayed teddy bear with the stuffings long hugged out of it.

"Lou, you're a sweetheart to offer, but I've got it under control." *Yeah, right, just like that time your Ivy League scholarship got revoked.* "I just hope Mr. Grey doesn't decide to fire me." She darted a furtive glance at the empty stage. "Is he gone?"

"Slick? Hell no, he ain't gone—this here's where he lives. And he ain't about to fire you, I guarantee it."

"You're sure?" she asked, taking hope.

"He ain't no Goody Two-shoes but—"

"Thought you'd flown the coup, Lou. You're not drinking up my profits are . . . you?"

Neil's eyes squinted as he took in the state of the bar. His surroundings had been no more than a blur while he'd been onstage. His energy had been concentrated on performing—and ignoring the redhead who he'd hoped would be gone by the time he left the office. Since the interview she'd been stuck on his brain like a needle grooved into a record.

He was beat and disgusted after tallying up the night's take and splitting the profits. Christine had another check on its way to L.A.

And a whole new set of dart holes right between the eyes.

"Must've been a real animal party I missed. Looks like a frat-house keg orgy minus the stripped-off togas."

"Mr. Grey, please, I can explain—"

"Aw, quit your stewin', Neil. Give the poor chile a break. Cain't you see—"

"What I see, Lou, is that it's time you headed home to Liza. Catch you on the flip side?"

As Neil closed the distance, he saw Lou pat Andrea's pale hands and whisper something before turning and sending him a distinct, silent message. Big Daddy was the best piano player around, and if the young upstart didn't give the little gal a break, Nimble Fingers was taking a powder.

As the two men slapped palms, Lou muttered, "Watch yo' mouth and mind yo' manners. Ain't all women bad. Cut her some slack, Slick."

"You giving me a choice?"

"Sho' I am. Be nice or be sorry. You got an ax to grind fo' sho', but it's wearin' thin on them who don't deserve it. Behave."

Neil grimaced as he locked up behind Big Daddy. The only real daddy he'd ever had, the man who took him off the streets. Mentor and friend, the old giant seldom made demands, but when he did, Neil always gave in.

"Rough night?" he asked as he strode behind the bar—and promptly stepped on a cherry. Looking down, he saw the spilled liquor and shuddered. What he was seeing was a waste of food and money, and that was a sin he couldn't abide.

"I'm really sorry, Mr. Grey." The wide eyes pleading for his understanding and the mussed hair that looked as though a thousand fingers had raked it overrode the memory of his childhood poverty. He put his anger on hold. "I know it's a mess, but I did my best. You can dock my salary for however much you lost tonight."

He couldn't help but respect the woman for making such an offer. Life had made him mean, but he prided himself on being fair.

"Don't sweat it. The fill-in I called didn't show?"

"Take a look and guess."

He did look. At her. Even frazzled, she had a

certain spark he could have related to ten years and a lifetime ago.

"Give me my week, and I promise to make this up to you."

Neil studied her determined, fervent expression and saw himself begging for a gig. She reminded him of himself when he'd been a kid, with dreams and ambitions and enough stupidity to believe in great beginnings and happy endings. Just looking at her made him feel wasted and angry for it. And jealous for some of what she had that he'd lost along the way.

"I won't leave until it's clean," she rushed on in the taut silence. "The register's already been emptied, so there's no reason for you to stay. I'll lock up when I'm through."

She reached for an overfilled ashtray, and he knocked it away. Her breath audibly caught, and she took a step back. Her eyes—Lord were they gorgeous—darted uneasily to his. So, he made her nervous. Dandy. He supposed that made them somewhat even.

"Aw, no no, *chère*," he said, his voice as smooth as the worn leather flask he pulled from his back pocket. "What kind of man do you take me for? I wouldn't dream of leaving you all alone. Lots of dangerous sorts roaming around this time of night, and you such a sweet thing. I insist on offering my protective presence, seeing that I'm not only generous but a gentleman."

He saw her swallow, but when she spoke, her words were steady. "I can take care of myself, thank you, Mr. Grey. If you'll excuse me, I have enough work to last me until daybreak. No need to worry about the 'dangerous sorts' on my behalf. See you tomorrow at five? Sharp."

Seemed that she could take care of herself, he thought, admiring her nerve and wishing he didn't.

"Trying to get rid of me? I'm hurt." The small snort she made told him she doubted he was capable of that emotion under any circumstances. Strangely enough, he was a bit stung. First honest-to-God twinge of personal injury he'd felt in a long, long time. "You don't think I can hurt, do you?"

"Can you?"

Neil frowned and uncapped the flask. There had been a sudden eagerness in her question that smacked of a newshound sniffing his tracks. Those story-mongers couldn't get it through their shifty heads that Neil Grey was old news. Sure the new and diehard fans paid their respects, along with the big-draw hotshots who needed his compositions to stay that way. But his recording career was *dead*. A fact that only seemed to fuel the public's fascination, as if he were an artist who'd died in his prime while his mystique lived on.

Tilting the flask to his lips, he paused. As many times as he'd been burned by the press, he wasn't taking chances. He'd make nice with Andrea, maybe tantalize her a tad, and find out in his own way whether she was up to no good.

"Make you a deal. I'll tell you. For a price."

She suspiciously eyed the flask that he'd extended.

"Name your price, and I'll decide if knowing's worth it."

"Best deal you ever cut, *chère*. I want four things from you. One: Join me for a drink. Two: Quit calling me Mr. Grey. Three: Tell me what brought you to the Big Easy when that accent of yours pegs you as a damn Yankee. And four: I could go for a good-morning kiss, and I'm willing to work hard to earn it. What do you say we pitch in together to clean up this hellacious mess, and then I'll see you home safe? Then, after that kiss, I'll answer your question. Deal?"

Andrea wondered if she'd actually heard right.

She'd braced herself for a request to join him for another dart game. Or a threesome—him, her, and his sax, since his ex-wife had told reporters she'd caught him sleeping with it once.

In fact, Andrea had anticipated anything but his offer of help, good-humored camaraderie, and concern for her safety. Those were rare commodities in her life that she'd long quit expecting to find. And she most certainly hadn't expected them from the man who'd been called schizophrenic by the tabloids.

Nostalgia stirred, and bad as it was for the super scoop she wanted, she hoped that she, and his many detractors, had misjudged him.

"The first three are fine . . . Neil. But that last one—"

"Aw, c'mon, Andrea. Be a good sport. Let me help clean up. And it would surely be my pleasure to walk you home."

"I'm talking about the kiss, and don't think for a minute I'm buying that innocent act of yours," she said sternly when he gasped dramatically. "*Just* a kiss? Uh-huh."

"*Just* a kiss, nothing else. On my mother's grave"—he took a quick swig from the flask, wiped his mouth with his forearm, then held out the brandy—"I swear it."

"Why do you want to kiss me?" she pressed, still not believing him.

"Because I like to kiss, and I pride myself on being a connoisseur of mouths. They're all different, but yours is more different than most, and I'd really appreciate the chance to sample the contents. Nothing personal. I'm only looking to expand my résumé. Surely, *you* can understand that."

Her lips twitched with amusement. And anticipation. A kiss from Neil Grey? Mr. Hot Lips himself, whose signed glossy she'd drooled over while the other kids at the orphanage had gone wild over rock-and-roll musicians, and for whom she'd dared to turn the radio dial from a Top 40 station to a jazz station? *He* wanted to kiss *her*?

"How is my mouth different?" And whose mouth had she inherited? Her mother's, her father's? One answer she'd never get. "Is it a good different or a bad different?"

"Hmmm. Let's see. Open your lips a tad, *chère*. . . . That's perfect, just enough so I can see your teeth. Great teeth, by the way."

"Great?" she repeated, trying not to move her lips while he studied them with what seemed to be detached interest. "But they're spaced a little in the front. I wish I'd had braces growing up. They're—"

"Sexy, that's what. Damn sexy. There's just enough room for the tip of a tongue."

Lord, she hoped he didn't ask for a peek at her tongue. What he might say about it—and its erotic possibilities—could have her begging for his kiss right there and then.

He didn't. Instead, he slid a finger over her lips, and she felt her soft flesh quiver. Despite her urgent message to her tongue not to touch, it did. He tasted of salt skin flavored with liquor and smoke. He tasted delicious.

"Curious tongue too," he said huskily. "Active little critter. Definitely an asset. Goes real nice with about the finest set of lips I ever checked out."

Andrea pinched her lips together. He rubbed them with his thumb, then traced them with a feather-light stroke before pulling back with a satisfied nod.

"Good muscle tone," he pronounced. "What's the longest kissing session you ever had?"

"Well, I've never timed one, but maybe half an hour, forty-five minutes?" She was suddenly ready for the drink he'd offered, though she already felt rather woozy.

"Practice makes perfect, and with such an incredible mouth, you should've had more practice than that. Stingy kissers who want to cut the fine art short rank with quitters and cheats in my book. How about you? Did you ever want to keep kissin' when some *monsieur* got antsy to move things along?"

"Well . . . yes. How did you guess?"

"I know men. *And* I know women. There's a reason why they're crazy about me. Tell the truth. You think it's the fame and fortune and a chance to get into my dancin' pants that have quite a reputation to please—or so said something I read. Used it for toilet paper, though I had a full roll."

If it hadn't been for his slow, easy smile, she would have thought he was testing her. But he seemed to be laughing at himself and inviting her to join him. Maybe that was the source of his brash but fatal appeal.

"Those reasons would be plenty for a lot of women."

"Don't I know it. But it's not reason enough for the ones with class and character. You've got both, don't you *chère*?"

"I like to think so."

"Could be you fall into a special slot. Could be you're one of those gals Lou keeps prattling about, who care more for kissin' than what it'll get 'em in the long run. A very rare breed."

"You sound cynical."

"Got good reason to be."

"I also get the impression that you like to kiss."

"Well, if you're not a genius and a dog groomer too. I'm a fool for kissing. Haven't met a woman yet who could outlast me. But I'd thank you for the opportunity to try you out."

Their fingers touched as she grasped the flask. He didn't let go. The sustained contact packed a hurricane punch. His lids lowered, and she thought he might try for a kiss without the promised preliminaries.

She wished that he would. If his kissing expertise half lived up to her expectations, she'd have a new facet of Neil Grey to write about—and just maybe she'd rediscover an old facet of herself in the process.

He didn't kiss her. But he did slide his fingers over hers and slowly urged the rim of the flask to her mouth.

Andrea pulled back. "We're in a bar, Neil, with a few clean glasses left."

"Are you that particular or just afraid of catching some social disease? Believe it or not, I'm cleaner than those glasses, and Lou's faithful to his wife, Liza. He's the only person I ever share with."

It was a challenge. His reputation over his word. Andrea debated, then made a choice. She never could stand cowards or liars—any more than quitters or cheats.

"I'm careful of the company I keep, Neil. And as far as I can tell, you and Lou are better than what I've had in a while. Why am I in the Big Easy instead of the Big Apple? It's all a calculated risk to make my life what I want it to be. I'm here because that's my choice. And so is my decision to accept your deal."

"Yowzah, I knew there was a reason besides great lips and great . . . um, great conversation that attracted me to you. My own choices haven't been anything to whistle Dixie about in the past, but according to Scarlett, tomorrow is another day. Maybe you'll prove her *and* Lou right. If you don't . . . here's to a little more pain shoveled onto the heap."

His coarse laughter doused her impression that he spoke from the gut. Andrea put the flask to her lips. The rim was still wet from his mouth. A vulgar mouth, a sensual mouth, out of which came revelations she was sure no reporter had been privy to before.

She felt like a cheat, and it didn't set well.

Neither did the brandy.

As she coughed and sputtered, she felt his palm

slap between her shoulder blades, then lessen to a gentle stroke.

"Does a body almost as much good as harm, huh, *chère*? Sorry about tonight. I'll make sure you don't get dumped on again. My fault. Not yours. Take another nip, and let's get to work. The sooner we're out of here, the sooner I can collect on that kiss."

Three

The first rays of sun slitted through a hung-over sky as the second order of *beignets* arrived at their Café du Monde table and their cups of *café au lait* were refilled for the fourth time. The creamy brew of chicory coffee and steamed milk was hot, but nothing like the scorcher the mid-May day promised to be.

Neil stretched, luxuriating in being a paying customer. He could remember scrounging for scraps in the café's trash cans while a train, whose tracks ran a spitting distance away, blew its midnight whistle down his back. The cook had found him out and had snuck him fresh *beignets* and glasses of milk, along with whatever change he could spare. It made Neil feel real good to send his benefactor an anonymous payback each month. Yessir, Neil Grey was a filthy-rich man. And just as he never forgave those who crossed him, he never forgot those who showed a kindness.

Those were the rules. And he did take pride not only in being in a position to set them, but in abiding by them as well. How he had come up in the world, sitting here next to a class-act woman.

The fans overhead circulated the thick, humid air,

while Neil watched Andrea bite into the hollow pastry known as a *beignet*. Powdered sugar dusted her cute upturned nose. He didn't mention it. Went nicely with her freckles. He liked them. He liked *her*—too much.

She took another bite of the messy French dough-nut, which she held gingerly. Neil chuckled, amused by her efforts not to get her fingers too sticky though she looked as if she wanted to suck them clean.

He'd like to see her suck a crawdad head, get her to forget those proper manners and cut loose. Hell, who could have a stompin' good time if they were gonna be prissy?

"You like those things, do you?"

"Mmmm, Neil, they are out of this world. I hate to admit it, but lately I've been having trouble getting into my jeans. I blame it on finding this place the first day I moved here, and a disgusting lack of self-control when it comes to sweets."

An image of her lying on a bed to pull up a zipper caused him to shift in his chair. He'd like to tell her that he was sweet in hopes she'd try a bite of him, but that would be about the biggest lie he'd ever told, and he had a disgusting lack of self-control when it came to dealing with liars.

"And how long have you been here?"

"Um . . ." She lingered over a sip of coffee. "Two weeks."

"Did you come to see friends and decide to stay?"

"No friends." She looked away, then suddenly smiled. *Whoooee.* When she smiled like that, he did believe the sun couldn't compete with the heat she generated. "At least, no friends to begin with. It seems that I've made a couple recently. You and Lou are really nice people."

"Lou's nice, unless you cross him. I learned not to do that years ago. As for me . . ." He'd suckered her in so far, but, good sport that he was, she deserved a reminder of just who she was in cahoots with. "I'm anything *but* nice, *chère*. Best you remember that for your own good."

Maybe she wasn't as smart as he'd given her credit for, smiling like that. Neil frowned. Something stinging and none too comfortable was going on in his chest. Must be heartburn. Nothing a belt of booze and a few smokes wouldn't get rid of.

She caught his wrist when he started to light up.

"Aw, crap," he muttered around his unlit cigarette. "Don't tell me you're one of those do-gooders looking for a lost cause to save. Let me guess which sermon I'm about to hear. I shouldn't smoke since it makes my lungs look like tar, and I oughtta get this coffin nail out of my mouth, right?"

"Hardly. As far as I'm concerned, it's your body, not mine, and you have every right to abuse it however you decide. As I said before, I believe in freedom of choice."

"Then *what*?" he grumbled, put out because her fingers wrapped around his wrist felt so fine, he didn't care if he never got this cigarette going.

"It's about what you said, that you were anything but nice. If you were all that bad, all that *slick*, you wouldn't have warned me. Neil."

She wrapped his name around her tongue in a whisper. He didn't much care for the effect it had on him, making his case of heartburn worse. He liked it even less when she took the matches away, along with her grip. His arm prickled as though it were being stuck with needles.

When she struck the match and leaned closer to light his cigarette, the prickling spread until his whole body felt like one giant pincushion.

Neil pulled back and took several deep drags. He felt very odd at the moment, not at all himself. This little gal was turning out to be more dangerous than he'd feared. Actually making him forget the Vow:

Women. Use 'em and lose 'em. Take them to bed, but never get inside their conniving heads. Slip into their skin, but never go deep enough to touch their cheating hearts.

The Vow. He'd kept it long before that night he'd checked into a seedy motel and played Russian roulette with a handgun. If he hadn't taken a guzzle every time the click went off without sending a bullet through his brain, then passed out until Lou found him, he supposed he wouldn't be sitting here now.

Sitting here and forgetting his vow. Life was a nasty game, and he'd learned that to survive, a man made his own rules. And here he was, forsaking his cardinal code.

A surge of the anger that ran soul-deep erupted when Andrea patted his hand as if he were some kind of good ol' boy she trusted. And then she had the gall to grin with delight as she wiggled her powdered-sugar fingers and stuck one in her mouth. The too-sensual mouth he greatly resented her for making him want.

Neil grabbed her wrist and jerked out her finger. He was pleased when the rest of her body seemed to jerk as well, then went still. Her breath came shallow and fast, and damn those eyes that searched his in confusion instead of returning his biting-hard glare.

She didn't resist as he pulled her hand forward, and he damned her for that because he wanted a struggle, an excuse to vent his rage. How he'd prefer the feel of her palm cracking against his cheek while he laughed and walked away. His mama had deserted him. Christine had betrayed him. They'd taught him only too well that the reigning champ left first.

How he'd prefer that. Not this trust, such stupid trust. She watched him take the cigarette from his mouth and poise the glowing red tip near her palm while he cinched her wrist.

"Never, *never* think that you know me better than I know myself, *enfant*," he whispered. "I won't be warning you anymore, so be smart and be careful of me."

He smiled coldly when her eyes took on a moist sheen and her mouth trembled. Good, she'd do them both a favor and tell him never to dare touch her again. She'd run off, just as he had, refusing the same kind of torture he'd suffered at his old man's hands in a roach-infested hovel.

"If you're planning to put that cigarette out on my palm, you'd better do it fast, because it's nearly burned down to the butt, and you're getting ashes in my coffee."

Good God, what kind of woman was he tangling with? Neil tongued the chip in his front tooth as her eyes began to look wetter, her mouth trembled even more, and his heartburn started feeling closer to a heart attack.

He dropped the cigarette into her cup. But he didn't let go of her wrist. Slowly, so slowly, he counted ten heartbeats to give himself time to come to his senses.

Closing his eyes, he pressed his lips to her palm. Her muffled moan echoed her taste. Sweet and good.

The gathered fingers he led into his mouth tasted even sweeter and—too bad for them both—better than good.

He groaned. And sucked them deeper, thrusting his tongue between the grooves, oblivious to the sparse company at other tables who didn't give a damn about them anyway.

He gave a damn. For the first time since he'd mistaken lust for love, he gave a damn. And with each lick he gave her a reason to give a damn, too, and court catastrophe with him.

"Do you kiss nearly as well?" she asked unevenly when he finally had the sugar lapped clean. At least four times. He had a thing about fours. Four was his lucky number, and he'd rather forget for now that lucky wasn't always what it seemed.

"You tell me once I get you home." When she

pushed back her chair, he beat her to it. Mama might have left him, but her teachings still ran true.

Gone were the blurry eyes and trembling chin. Andrea had some kind of glow inside that was turning his insides to mush. Then she smiled as if they shared a secret about him, and that secret was safe with her.

It infuriated him, excited him. There she was, the girl next door sitting in for Vanna White, challenging him to go for broke with a single letter. *A* . . . was for *adultery*. *B* . . . for *betrayal*. *C* . . . was for *commanding* himself to switch the channel to *Let's Make a Deal* and choose the mystery door. He knew he had less to lose than she did by taking the chance.

Unfortunately for her, he'd always had a weakness for science fiction and *Father Knows Best*. Anything that promised an escape from what he knew to be real.

She couldn't be for real. Which was fine, considering he didn't feel too real himself at present. Andrea was more potent than a whole flask of brandy.

By the time he'd insisted on paying the small bill and agreed to let her pick up the next tab with "the tips she was sure to earn," Neil was real worried about keeping the Vow.

They held hands that they swung between them. Leaning against each other, they ran fingers down the iron gates of the St. Louis Cathedral, the oldest cathedral in the United States. It had such history, something they didn't, but it didn't seem that way to Andrea. She knew they were still strangers, so why did she feel they were long-lost friends?

After tossing coins into a shoe-shine box without stopping for a shine, they ran like two thieves until they stopped, exhilarated and out of breath, in front of the crumbling building she called home.

The first place she'd ever called home.

It was hers for now, at a ridiculous price, and as they held on to the wobbly banister up three flights of stairs, past graffiti-covered walls, Andrea felt her anticipation grow. It wasn't just the promised kiss from this enigma who was nothing and everything like the man behind the music she'd expected to find. Humble though her apartment was, she was eager to show it to Neil.

They shared some kind of kinship she didn't understand. He did scare her at times, something she'd anticipated and steeled herself for, but there was a tragic and honest edge about him that she gravitated to. She instinctively trusted it. Enough to invite him into the place she made her own without fear he would renege on his promise of *just* a kiss.

"We're here," she said excitedly, fitting the key into her front door.

"I noticed the other doors have peeling paint. Mind if I ask why yours is missing the same distinction?"

"Because I painted it. And the landlord agreed to knock off a week's rent in exchange for me painting and cleaning the inside." She opened the door, enormously pleased with her accomplishment as she inhaled the scent of potpourri. "Isn't it cozy?" she asked, wanting his approval and not sure she was getting it as he looked around the one-room efficiency.

"It's . . . cozy, all right. Maybe a little too?"

"Not for me. And since I'm the one who lives here, what anyone else thinks really doesn't matter."

But it did. At least, what Neil thought mattered, even though she knew it shouldn't. She anxiously watched as he ran a finger along the fringe of a vintage shawl she'd draped over the French doors leading to the balcony. He spread a palm against a pane of glass, then clenched his fist tight, as if wanting to pound his way out. Instead, he pressed his forehead against the glass, then stepped away fast.

"I would have fixed it up anyway, but the landlord

didn't know that. I've learned to wheel and deal and make a dollar stretch. And that's fine, because I'm fond of my things, and making do doesn't bother me. It can even be fun, depending more on your imagination than what's in the wallet."

She couldn't seem to make herself quit talking, telling him what he might not even want to know. But even as he paced, he seemed to be listening, and it had been so long since she'd had someone she could talk to. When he traced a broken stained-glass window before moving to the shelf of knickknacks, she fought panic. He'd picked up a vintage picture frame and was studying it closely.

"It's like a game for me," she rushed on. "I have a thing for flea markets and—"

"Where'd you get this old publicity shot of me?" he demanded. "It's been out of circulation for a good ten years. Did you find it at a local flea market for, say, a dime?"

Andrea claimed it from him and held it to her possessively. Had she imagined the slight tremor in his hands?

"No, Neil, it's one of the few links to my past that I'm attached to. When I was thirteen, I joined your fan club. It cost me four dollars to join, and I spent an afternoon polishing floors to earn the money. I couldn't get off the school bus fast enough every day for a month to ask Sister if I'd gotten any mail."

"You must've been scraping, looking for junk mail."

"It wasn't junk mail to me," she said defensively. "When my packet finally came, with a forty-five record, a newsletter, and a personally autographed glossy, I was floating on air for days. Until one of my roommates scratched the record because she said she was sick of hearing it. I couldn't help but rub it in that her favorite movie had a Neil Grey sound track."

"Sorry about what I said." He cleared his throat. "I shouldn't have called your mail 'junk.' Even if that was and still is my opinion."

She accepted his gruff apology and decided to risk something of herself in hopes that he would do the same.

"I grew up in an orphanage, Neil. In Connecticut."

"Was it bad?"

"Not really. The sisters were good to us. They made do a lot too. I'm sure I missed a lot not growing up in a regular family, but I'm not sorry I learned to fend for myself. What I have, I earned. No one gave it to me. I take pride in that."

"You should. I respect survivors. Seems we've got some common ground in a quality I greatly prize."

She wondered if he would still respect her if he knew she'd moved to New Orleans for the express purpose of gaining access to him. Her grand plan to do an exposé on a legend in his own time, who remained a mystery to jazz scholars and enthusiasts, was unfolding better than she'd dared dream.

Only it was unfolding in unexpected curves and sharp angles and pulling her in with him when objectivity was essential in a fiercely competitive, self-taught profession. She wanted to be the best, the absolute best. Prove to herself and everyone else she wasn't a funny-toothed girl in secondhand clothes, a girl even her parents hadn't wanted.

Her resolve firm, Andrea repositioned the picture, then took his hand and led him to the faded maroon pullout sofa. She liked the way his fingers felt laced with hers. It sparked excitement, but she also felt comfort.

"I take it that you're a survivor too, Neil?"

"Guess you could say that. I'm frayed around the edges, something of a rough cut. But I'm doing what I always loved to do best. Creating. Performing on a honky-tonk stage."

"Shades of Grey isn't exactly a honky-tonk. It's a very classy place. Mahogany and brass and crystal. At least in the club itself. Your office is—"

"It isn't too fancy, but it's mine, the way I like it. Well lived in and a little scruffy. Like me."

Andrea held her breath, praying she'd sound casual while she spoke her next words.

"Tell me more about Neil Grey. Does he ever think about trading his office in for another shot at a career he quit while he was at the peak and his legion of listeners begged for more?" She felt his thigh stiffen against hers. And then she felt her own stiffen as his jaw worked back and forth.

"No," he said abruptly. "Gotta ashtray round here? I like using my floor, but nobody else's. One's crude, the other's rude. I like to think I know the difference between bad habits and bad manners. It's a fine line, like most else in the world, but Lou and Liza did their best to pick up where Mama left off. That in mind, could you get me one?"

"You mean your mother left, and Lou and Liza—?"

"Not that it's anybody's business, but Lou's my adoptive father. Ask me no questions, I'll tell you no lies. I've had enough of this nonsense. Either get me an ashtray or lose your security deposit. Another flick and this rug's toast."

"One ashtray on the way." Heart palpitating, Andrea commanded herself to be calm as she went to the cupboard and found the dainty crystal ashtray she'd bought for a song.

A roach ran over her hand as she reached for it.

"Ohmigod!" Jerking her hand back, she threw open the cabinet under the sink and rummaged around for the insecticide. As she grabbed it, she saw another roach skitter out and almost land on her feet.

Frantically, she began spraying. "Oh, these horrible creatures. I can't stand them. Get away, you nasty things! Take that! And that! And—"

Suddenly, she was staring at Neil's shoe. With a quick stomp he smashed two more roaches that were scrambling around.

He snatched the can away, threw it to the floor, and wrenched her from her knees. He held her arms so tight and the face she looked up to held such a fierceness, she wondered for a wild, horrible moment if he meant to start shaking her.

"I've got two things to say to you. First, you explain that snoopy question about my recording career. Why do you want to know?"

"Be-because—" Damn, dammitall to hell. Her teeth were chattering, and she couldn't make them stop. "Because I'm an old fan, that's why. A girl who grew up on your music and never forgave you for stopping. No one ever knew exactly what your background was, since your stories were always conflicting, but—but I told myself you made things up because maybe you were an orphan like me who wanted to reinvent your past. You made it big, and whenever I looked at your picture, I believed I could do it, too, that nothing could stop me."

"I didn't even sign the friggin' picture. You hear me? Some jerk I never met did all the signing, sent all that promo crap to poor little orphan girls who polished floors and sent their money to the greedy recording machine that almost ate me up before it spit me out."

Andrea commanded herself not to cower or run as he cursed vilely between harsh, ragged breaths.

But then she felt his hand, his large, warm hand, stroke softly through her hair while his other swept to her back.

He drew her against him, and it was such a desperate, needy embrace, she felt her fear change to an unknown emotion that pierced her chest. She felt quick kisses pressed to her forehead, her temple, heard his hoarse murmurs of apology for not signing the damn picture he'd always hated. Until he stilled and gently cupped her face.

"Andrea, *chère,* go home," he pleaded. His eyes refuted his words. "You're courtin' trouble if you stay here. I'm the trouble, and you won't be safe in the same city as me. I feel something for you, and that's risky—for us both." He released her and pulled out a folded stack of bills that he slapped into her palm, then flattened her fingers over. "Take this and buy a ticket on the next plane out to wherever you want to call home. Find a decent place to live. And don't come back. Keep your distance from me, and keep it good."

Four

Andrea stared at the most money she'd ever seen in her life and felt a sinking sensation in the pit of her stomach. Her back still tingled where he'd touched and where his lips had brushed—she felt as if she'd been kissed by an angel. He claimed to be the Devil's own, and yet he'd sought to protect her from himself.

She could leave, shake the New Orleans dust and Neil Grey from feet that were tired of ceaseless wandering. With no roots—no longed-for roots—she had no reason to stay.

And if she stayed? She'd get more than the story she'd come for. She'd be plunged even deeper into an array of emotions and excitement that felt forbidden, thrilling. A rush.

A dangerous rush skating the edge of darkness.

"Keep your money, Slick. I'm not keeping my distance." As if the cash were something foul, she crammed it back into his pants pocket, her fingertips wedging between smooth fabric and the pelvis beneath it.

"In that case . . ." He locked her hand where it was before she could pull away. "I'm giving you a final warning: You're stuck with your decision—a very foolish decision at that. We're gonna take each other on, *chère*. Should be interesting to find out if either of us leaves in one piece. Does that give you a fair idea of what you've gotten yourself into?"

She had difficulty swallowing, her throat was so dry. What *had* she gotten herself into? Probably more than a prudent woman would have bitten off. But she had and didn't regret it—yet. For now she had more than one reason to stay. Neil wasn't just a byline. He was a man who made her want.

"It seems I remember agreeing to a good-morning kiss. *Just* a kiss." She stared as he slid her palm inside his pants pocket back forth over taut muscle and hard bone. It was then that she saw the strain even his baggy trousers couldn't disguise.

"Like what you see, *chère*?"

He laughed low when she forced her gaze to his face. Forced, because she not only liked what she saw, she didn't want to relinquish the quickening arousal she felt, the sensual excitement she'd feared was gone forever. Stolen by an old lecher's cloying breath and grasping gnarled hands, she joyfully, greedily, reclaimed what was hers to explore, to respect, to share. And to fear.

The need Neil stirred was too intense. Too unfamiliar. It was an achingly personal revelation, and the cause of it only increased her delight and distress with his sexy smile.

"You're damn cute when you turn that pretty shade of pink. Think I'll write some music for you— long time since a woman inspired me to do that. 'Andrea.' Great title. Maybe you'll hear your name on the radio one day."

"You mean you might cut another release?" She grasped at the exciting prospect. Almost as exciting as the feel of his hand stroking hers near the place she commanded herself not to stare at again. Not to touch. "You'd do that for me?"

"Sorry to shoot down your hopes, but I wouldn't do that for anybody. I write the music; other artists buy the rights to my songs. My days of touring and cutting hits are gone. No major recording company with a stitch of sense'll touch me. Been that way for five years. Or didn't you know?"

"What I know is that you could be even greater now than you were when I sent in my four bucks." She knew better than to push, but she was feeling brave. If she could come to terms with her past, why couldn't he? Whatever his real past might be. "You're better than ever, Neil. What the Beatles were to rock when they broke up, what Hank Williams was to country when he died, you are to jazz—"

"*Was*," he insisted, as if his denial could make it true. "I'm a has-been at a young age, if you're counting years. I had my moment, rising up fast as a phoenix before I crashed and burned. No campfire, *chère*, we're talkin' a major meltdown. It'd take a miracle to raise me from the ashes."

"But the cinders glow brightly. You could find an independent label and pick up where you left off. A lot of people are hoping that will happen. I'm one of them."

"Lots of people, including you, aren't me. I stared so long at the sun, I was all but blinded. I'm where I'm at now by choice, Andrea. Try to understand that. And if you can't, accept it as fact. Take it from me—if you're not good for your own person, you're not good for nobody."

"And are you . . . good for yourself?"

"Not by a long shot, so you can imagine where that puts others. Especially you."

"I thought you weren't giving me any more warnings."

"Not a warning, a promise. And promises are something I always keep." He wedged her hand farther into his pocket. "You got past the first hurdle, and I'm satisfied you're not a lowlife, diggin' for dirt nosy newshound. So let's get down to the second item of business. I want you out of here. Broken windows. Roaches the size of gutter rats. I want to set you up someplace you can walk home by your lonesome without me frettin' you're getting there safe before I come to call."

"It's certainly no worse than your office," she countered, stung. And shocked enough by his blatant demand to set her up—*did he actually think she would agree to be his kept woman*—that his insult to her profession was forgotten.

"My office isn't where I lay me down to sleep. Get your bags packed, *chère*. You're out of here."

"I most certainly am not packing my bags. And you don't have to worry about where I sleep, because I won't be sleeping with you!" She jerked her hand out of his pocket and away from his grip fast. He made no move to get it back.

"Not yet. But you will, and I'll make sure you love every minute of it. Until then, and there will be a *then*, I'm getting you out of this hovel and into a decent place. These are the facts: I like you—way too much. I desire you even more. But neither are enough for me to sleep down memory lane."

"And just where do you suggest that I move to? Don't tell me—your private quarters. I've heard that song and dance before, Neil. You were right, I was foolish. Foolish enough to hope for better from you."

"You get better than that from me, so wipe that hurt look off your face. I don't like it no more than this hellhole."

"How—how arrogant," she sputtered, searching for words, which were her stock-in-trade, only to come up with nothing sufficient to express her disdain. "I can't believe you coming in here and running down what I've worked for—worked *hard* to call mine. How would you like it if I spit on your sax or tore up your musical scores?"

"Nothing that nobody else hasn't already done," he said blandly. "*Chère*, it looks like we're already off at the starting gate. Slow start, but let's see how fast you learn. Hit me with something harder if you aim to make a dent."

He grinned. She couldn't believe it! He was enjoying this, baiting her, toying with her as if she were some kitten batting at the string he held and had complete control of.

She'd never been this mad in her life, so mad she completely forgot her gratitude for him making her want the very thing he was suggesting. Neil Grey was going to find out she didn't come running when any man crooked his finger.

Neil would be lucky to still have his when he left.

"Apparently, *Slick*, your bad habits and even worse manners need to learn a lesson about me. You might call the shots at work, but I call my own shots wherever I claim my turf. This is my turf, Neil. And you're no longer welcome. I'm not for sale. Repeat: *Not . . . for . . . sale.* Go find someone else to lay yourself down to sleep with, because I'd rather rot in a pine box than share sleazy pillow talk with you."

His brow lifted in amusement as he slowly clapped his hands.

"I'm impressed, very impressed. I knew you had some gumption, but I was afraid to hope for this much. Feels good, don't it? All that sizzle pumping up your insides, a real adrenaline rush. Best sex I ever had was always after tearing into an opponent before we tore up the sheets. Too bad we've got more lessons to swap before slipping between some of our own. In other, more inviting quarters, mind you. With flowers, champagne, music. I always was a sucker for romance."

Was the man deaf, dumb, and blind? And what did he think he was doing, stretching with a big, lazy yawn before snapping the suspenders over his chest, then shrugging them off so that they hung provocatively from his lean waist to his thighs?

"Get out!" Andrea pointed a shaking finger at the door. "Did you hear me? I said, *Get out.* Take your

inflated ego, along with your obnoxious proposi-
tions, out the door with you."

"Be happy to," he drawled. "After I get my kiss.
Just a kiss, the way we agreed. Pucker up, *chère*. The
sooner we get this over with, the sooner you'll see my
back."

"You don't actually believe I'm willing to let you—"

"Of course I do. We did strike a bargain, so it's a
done deal as far as I'm concerned. And remember
that cheats aren't allowed to work for me. One kiss
and I promise you'll eat your words."

It had been almost seven years since she'd desired
a man, and her need to excel went even longer and
deeper than that. She had a story to write, one that
was bigger than his ego, and she would best him at
his own game.

She had to keep the job to do it. And if that meant
giving him a kiss, then she was back in the race.
She'd give him a kiss that would make him eat her
dust and out of her hand.

"Okay, Neil, have it your way. Take your kiss, then
get out, and I'll see you at five. Sharp."

"You want to do it here with the roaches? Or on the
couch that's likely filled with bedbugs?"

"I'll take vertical over horizontal with you any day."

"If you say so. Just remember that you can always
change your mind, and I'm going to do my damndest
to see that you do."

"Another final warning, Neil? You're damaging
your credibility, not to mention exhausting your
supply of—"

He suddenly pressed himself against her, and she
caught at the countertop cutting into the small of her
back. His groin was anchored into her feminine
juncture, and though she could have easily tossed
him into the sink, the urge to do just that was
nothing compared to her urge to tilt and rub.

"*Bing*. The second round's started. Get ready,
chère. We'll see who makes it to the final ring."

She opened her mouth to retaliate, but her words were swallowed by his own open mouth. The words she sought to form were pushed back by the force of his tongue. He sucked and worked his lips and tongue in a fluid, energetic ballet that would have been brutal had it not been performed with the artful beauty of a master. All the while he sinuously stroked her errant arms, which embraced him.

As soon as her lips were loose and eager, he gentled the kiss and began to explore her teeth. The tip of his tongue traced the tiny spaces she'd always hated . . . until now. They became erotic treasures he leisurely wooed, making her feel they were a unique part of her that he saw beauty in.

He ran a thumbnail up and down her spine until she arched. Her hips rose to meet his slow bump and grind. She thrust her hands through his hair, the feel of it as silky and thick as his tongue mating with hers. Vaguely, she realized that he must have been right. The anger she'd felt was transforming into passion, becoming an uncivilized raw hunger. Gone was any thought of restraint or a get-even strategy.

She had to touch him. *Had to.* The desire was so strong, it was as though she was driven by a merciless compulsion. But when she insinuated her palm between their undulating torsos, he yanked it away and placed it firmly on the countertop.

"A kiss," he hissed against her lips. "*Just* a kiss so long as you live here. Take it, *chère.* Take it and want more. Because you're not getting more till I have my way."

Her whimpered protest met with his laughter.

She had no idea how long it went on, but it must have been close to an hour. And then she couldn't bear the unfilled emptiness anymore. She tore her swollen mouth from his and cried out in agonized defeat at his refusal to let her fully claim a womanly triumph.

Neil's hand stroked her from throat to breast to

open thighs. He cupped the juncture of those thighs, fingers pressed in and rubbing.

"Just a kiss," he taunted softly. She just missed the peak as he took his hand back and sealed her in a voracious embrace. His lips swept from her scalp to her chin in the sweetest afterplay, while she continued to shake and all but weep. "I cheated, just a tad. Sorry 'bout that. Didn't mean to get carried away. Best damn kiss I've had in years. Maybe even the best ever. Thanks for expanding my résumé."

She was still high, but painfully unfulfilled as she reached out, only to grasp nothing. Not even his arms. He was almost at the door. *How could he leave her like this?*

"You bastard," she gasped, striding toward him and grabbing his arm. "You damn *slick* bastard. You're manipulative, selfish—"

"I'm all that," he said. "And more. Definitely *more* at the moment." He caught her wrist and brought her hand to his straining fly. "Don't believe me? Put those nails in my skin to better use, and feel *this*."

He felt . . . alive, vitally male. She clenched him. And as she did, the ugly, withered thing etched into her memory was altered to a form that was healthy, virile, sleek, and hard.

Neil pried away her searching fingers and pulled back.

Hands off. Bodies separated. A foot between them while they glared at each other and struggled for breath.

"See you at five, *chère*. Try to get some rest. This was nothing compared to what's in store."

He pulled the door open, but she slammed it shut.

"I never liked a cheat either, Neil. I kept my end of the bargain—now it's your turn to ante up. You never answered the first question. Do you ever hurt?"

"You still have to ask? I'm hurting. *Bad*. Look between my legs if you want proof."

"What I want is an answer from your past. Your heart."

"My heart?" he repeated derisively. "You mean what's left of it? So little left I don't have one."

"I don't believe that."

"You don't *want* to believe it, that's your problem. Right now I've got a problem of my own I aim to satisfy."

"You're leaving here to go to a prostitute?"

"Don't *ever* suggest such a thing to me again. I have standards—hot damn, can you believe it?—as to who I screw. And *where* I screw them."

"I don't screw," she said between clenched teeth.

He looked her over, several times, before a slow, smug smile spread from his lips, lips that were incredible and, despite everything, still vastly desirable. Worst of all, he knew it.

"We'll see about that. Should be fun changing your mind. Even if you're in need of a few pointers, I'll be more than happy to oblige." He tweaked her nose. "Later, *chère*."

"You cheat! You double-crossing cheat! Do you hurt? *Can* you hurt? Tell me or this is the last deal we ever cut."

His smirk disintegrated.

"Can I hurt?" he repeated distantly, his eyes turning into mires of desolation. "First, answer me this. Why do you think artists are driven to do what they do? Why do painters tell a story with drawings or writers paint a picture with words? Give you a hint. The same reason musicians express themselves in a language that speaks to strangers."

"Because . . . because they're compelled to express their emotions? Or it's their way of filling an empty spot inside?"

"That's a good part of it, but not all. The pain, *chère*. They work from the pain. The kind that hurts and never goes away. But no real artist wants it to, since that's the emotionally poisoned well they draw from. The more it hurts, the better they can be. Think of Van Gogh, Edgar Allan Poe, more actors than you can count, and . . . *me*."

"Then you must hurt deeply," she said softly, recognizing his wise, jaded strength, feeling an empathy with him that even her resentment couldn't deny.

He reached for her, and though she cursed herself for it, she clung to him. The steady beat of his heart thumped against her cheek as she heard him sigh.

"I do. But, *chère*, it hurts so good."

Five

Andrea locked her apartment door, barring any undesirable sorts that might have followed her home. She denied the immediate impulse to turn on every light and scanned the room by glow of the blinking neon sign outside. Assured she was alone, she hurried to the balcony and pulled back the gauzy curtains.

Frantically, she searched the street below. The bum she'd almost stepped on was still lying in the trash-strewn gutter. One of her neighbors, a female impersonator working at a local nightclub, stopped at a corner across the street and said something to someone in the shadows.

Was that the someone she'd felt dogging her steps home for the past week, only to disappear whenever she spun around? Or was it only her imagination making the fine hair prickle on her neck? Each night when she'd reached her building, she sensed her stalker pause. Heart pounding, she'd flooded her apartment with light then yanked back the drapes in silent challenge, but whenever she peered out she saw . . . nothing.

This time she left the lights off, rendering herself as invisible as her night stalker. The thin curtain trembled in her grip as she waited and watched. Her neighbor headed toward the apartment building. A match flared in the shadows, then went out.

A large man stepped forward.

Tilting up his head, he looked straight at her balcony.

Andrea let go of the curtain and pressed her back to the wall, her heart racing. *Neil.* She peeked out again and saw that he glanced at his watch, took several cigarette puffs, then strode in her direction.

Was he trying to scare her away or scare her back, since all week she'd been keeping a safe, not-within-touching distance from him?

Whichever it was, she was going to find out. She turned on the lamp beside her couch and prepared to do battle as she struggled with the stubborn lock on the French doors. It finally gave, and she stepped onto the balcony with a huff.

The sharp challenge on her tongue faltered when she found herself staring at his retreating back. She saw the somersault of his cigarette in the air, and then, like him, it was gone.

Andrea took several shaky breaths. And then she pulled out her portable typewriter from the closet. The sweat had yet to dry on her palms as she began to read her latest notes:

Who is this man really? What drives him to perform and yet shun applause from the masses, to create but let lesser artists revel in the glory of his compositions rather than take rightful claim?

These are a few of the contradictions defining Neil Grey. As a professional, he creates music that is beyond ambition. He captures the invisible grace note even auspicious peers miss. It's his signature, and no one can duplicate it, not even a master forger.

But as with Beethoven, it's a gift that seems misplaced in the hands of a man who shrugs off the honor, and those who would honor it. Many similarities exist between these two musical geniuses: the arrogance; self-centered egotism; foul mouths, and even fouler manners. But Grey's disdain is more subtle, and it is that subtlety that makes the pain he seems driven to share keener and more offensive.

Rereading the last paragraph, she felt her palms grow more moist. She typed *XXXX*. As many *X*'s as it took to silence a half hour's angry work that was anything but objective.

She began to pound the keys, putting one word in front of the other, until day broke and her back ached.

Andrea stretched and sighed as she read the new pages. She'd given up the vain quest for objectivity, but at least she had managed to be fair. Most of it would have to be rewritten, at least a page trashed, but the last paragraph she knew she'd keep:

He is the rarest of breeds, a visionary who casts a giant shadow but hides it to walk among men. He hides it well, and for reasons unknown—but his purpose, elusive like his music, is there. He is a rebel with a cause who likes to shake things up, then disappear to watch from the wings. . . .

It was dark, pitch-black, the way he liked it when he had something to think about. That's when the music usually came, with everything silent except for the melody filling his head.

Like a sparkler on the Fourth of July, the glowing red tip of Neil's cigarette slashed the air while his foot tapped to the beat.

"Dammit, and damn *her* while I'm at it. That's not it." He stopped the cigarette in mid-arc and swooped it to his mouth.

He breathed in the strong smoke and cursed her some more. Who did she think she was, getting under his skin and messing with his brain? He hoped she was satisfied; this was one of the worst dry spells he could remember since when.

If something didn't give and give soon, he wasn't going to be able to pack in pigs, much less a full house of paying guests. No one had to tell him—though Lou already had—that he wasn't up to snuff. He didn't have the same swagger onstage, and it didn't help matters that every time he glanced at the bar, his mouth went dry and his notes went flat.

Neil lit a smoke with the one he was about to crush. At this rate he wouldn't need to worry about overhead and Christine, since he'd have emphysema before the year was out.

Then again, maybe liver disease would get to him first.

As he reached into his back pocket, a soft knock sounded at the office door.

"Yeah?" he yelled. "Who is it and whaddaya want? Unless someone died, scram, 'cause it's gonna be your funeral."

The door cracked open, and a thin stream of light cast a slender silhouette onto the floor.

"Neil? I'm sorry to bother you, but Lou had to get home early and everyone else is gone." She paused as if waiting for a reply that didn't come. "I brought you the money from the cash register—the club manager was out, and you forgot to empty it when you closed up."

He didn't forget. He just hadn't wanted to get that close to his Achille's heel, and damn Lou, too, since he'd promised to bring the money himself.

The silence stretched long and thick between them, and even from where he sat, he could see her shift uneasily.

"Neil, the tray's getting a little heavy," she said, breathless. "Where should I put it?"

"On my desk."

"I can't see. Where's the light switch?"

"Leave it off and take your best shot. Proprietor's prerogative."

"But I'm afraid I'll trip and drop it."

"Trip, and I'll pick you up. Drop it, and we'll have more fun than scrambling for throws from a Mardi Gras float."

"If you insist, *boss.*" Gone was the soft tone; her voice was back to its hoity-toity clipped accents. "But if I do fall, don't bother to catch me. I can pick myself up." She added on a whisper he didn't think he was meant to hear, "Lots of practice."

He watched her move in while his mind cast about for some way to end their stalemate. That kiss had turned him inside out, but he couldn't bring himself to take back the rules she wanted nothing to do with. Some rules could be bent, most couldn't. He never made one without having a good reason to make it.

The cash box landed with a *thump* on his ledger.

"Care to take me on for a game of darts?" Dumb idea, but it was the first thing that came to him. "Darts in the dark. I get black, you get red. Forget the navel, we'll vie for either nipple or thereabouts. You rack up the most zaps, and I'll raise your wage. But if I win, you give me a kiss. Make it good enough, and I just might raise your wage anyhow."

"I don't think so, Neil. Catch me later, when I'm up to taking you on. I'm ready to crawl *alone* into my bedbug bed."

"Wait." He crushed out the cigarette and quickly got up. "I'll walk you home."

"No thank you," she said politely. So politely he wished she was back to calling him names. Then he'd have an excuse to be a bully again—only he'd be a slyer bully, one who knew she didn't take to ultimatums.

He beat her to the door. Shutting it, he sealed them in darkness. She was so close to his chest, his thighs, he felt her body heat, lush and defiant, mingle with his. Her scent was fresh and feminine, some lemon-and-lavender smell he'd never detected on any woman but her.

"Not even if I let you buy the *beignets* and coffee on

the way? You did offer, and I'm calling in my rain check."

"And I'm taking a rain check on the rain check."

He didn't know how to deal with her evasion. The shoe was on the other foot, and he didn't care for the fit.

"You don't seem to want my company. My 'inflated ego' takes exception to that. Tell the truth, *chère*. Afraid I might melt some of that ice you've wrapped around yourself? It's so thick I don't even pick up my own money for fear of frostbite."

"Careful, Slick. A woman might get the impression that she's managed to intimidate the master string-puller himself."

He stepped forward; she matched him with a back step.

"Either it works both ways or we're dancin' in the dark." Swiftly, he secured a hand at her waist. His other hand brushed a breast before sliding down her arm to grip the hand he expected was ready to take a swing.

"Didn't mean to touch you there, much as I want to. Dance with me?" He could feel her faint tremor as well as her stiffening spine. "I'll hum the tune I'm having trouble working out. I'd thank you for your help."

"Why do you think I can help?" There was a crack in the ice. He heard it in the soft shadows of her voice, the slight give of her tensed muscles. He pulled her closer.

"Because it's something I'm writing for you. And like you, it's driving me a little crazy because I know it's there, and it's incredible, only me and the muse are playing hide-and-seek. We're in synch for a few measures, but then it goes one way and I go another."

"Like last night . . . and every night since you laid down your terms and I exercised my right of refusal? You've been tailing me, Neil. Why?"

"Just getting my exercise. And making sure you get home in one piece while I'm at it. Got a problem with that?"

"Yes!" She gave a disgruntled snort, followed by a long sigh. "You scared me, Neil. Maybe you meant well, but you scared me all the same. I've lived in bigger towns and in worse neighborhoods, where I rode the subway alone after midnight. But never have I run into my apartment, fearing for my life. You should have asked to walk me home, the way you just did, instead of being so sneaky about it."

"But you turned me down—the same reason I saved my breath before. Didn't mean to scare you, Andrea. If you'd told me you thought you were being followed, I would've 'fessed up. And *then* walked you home. Whether you liked it or not."

"Don't tell me Neil Grey's appointed himself some kind of guardian angel after he made sure I realized, in no uncertain terms, that he's no more than a fastidious devil on the make. Which one are you, Slick?"

Neil leaned against the door as he tightened his hold and pulled her, unresisting, with him. Lord, but she did feel good. Too damn good. The woman was turning him to mush, a disgusting, quivering heap of male flesh that had never felt anything like this in his entire rags-to-riches life.

"Which one am I? When it comes to you . . . some of both—not that I like it. I worry about you being on the streets alone at night. But I do want to make it with you, in the worst sort of way. I'm a helluva lot more comfortable with the second than the first. Big surprise, huh?"

"I'll tell you what the big surprise is: discovering you're concerned about my well-being when I haven't exactly been Miss Congeniality."

"That's putting it mildly. You've had a smile for everybody but me. The only looks I've gotten from you—when you've even bothered to look—could shrivel prunes."

She laughed softly, a breezy wisp of sound that tickled his ears, while her breath, which smelled faintly of cloves and cinnamon, teased his nose. He breathed her in, and his brain whirled while his hormones forgot he was way beyond getting turned on by a scent and the feel of a woman's covered breasts against his chest.

"Then I suppose I made my point, and I can put my voodoo doll away," she said. "I'll be sure to take out the pins before I go to sleep tonight."

"Don't tell me you bought one of those damn things. A person can't even go into a convenience store anymore without seein' those ugly little monsters, and— Where did you stick those pins, anyway?"

"Let's see . . . I gave you cavities and toe fungus and jock itch. Sorry, Neil. I was mad."

"Guess I'm lucky you didn't give me impotence too."

"Um . . . I did."

Neil chuckled. "Didn't work, *chère*."

"Obviously," she said, a bit shyly, but also pleased. Before he could sort out the impact that particular combination had on his senses, she changed the subject. "Now, about that tune you're writing for me—"

"We'll get to that. First, you tell me something. When you came in here tonight, I got the feeling— just for a bit—that you might be willing to call a truce. Were you?"

"It was my original intention. Lou was going to bring you the money, but I asked him to let me. 'More power to ya, chile' were his words, I believe. He also said that he knew you weren't the easiest man to put up with, but there were reasons for that, and a smart gal like me would put aside her grievances long enough to find out why, because 'underneath all that ugly meanness, there do be a whole lotta soul.'"

Neil scowled. He didn't appreciate Lou playing matchmaker by touting qualities of his that no longer existed. Then again, he wasn't yet in a position to give up the few points he'd scored with Andrea. By the time they played it out—why did that certainty suddenly make him wish for a swig?—she'd realize Lou had sold her a bill of rotten goods.

But he'd let her find that out for herself. For some crazy reason he needed her, and he planned to keep her around for as long as he could.

"Then if you came up here, sympathizin' with my troubled waters, why did you change your mind and get nasty with me?"

"You got nasty when I came in, so I gave you a dose of your own medicine to see how you liked the taste. Force of habit, Neil. You've got your bad habits, I've got mine."

"Was it force of habit that had you turning me down when I offered my strollin' company? You could've taken it even further than that. Maybe set me up by making a quick date with one of those regulars I've seen slipping you their numbers and getting too chummy with you for my liking."

She laughed that laugh again, only this time it didn't meet with his appreciation. This time it took another whack at his masculine pride.

"Don't tell me you're actually . . . *jealous*?"

Jealous—*him*? Certainly not. Only fools who let a woman dicker with their insides felt such nonsense.

The kind of nonsense he'd been cursing himself for all night and every night that he'd followed her to see that she wasn't just getting home safely, but alone.

"You've had plenty of smiles for them and none for me," he growled. "If you'd been of a mind to do more than stick pins into a voodoo doll tonight, you might've hooked up with one of those eager beavers, all the time laughing that pretty little laugh of yours while you knew I watched around a dark corner."

"Why would I do something like *that*?"

The million-dollar question he couldn't answer. He only knew it had to do with greed and betrayal. The price paid when a man let success seduce him into giving everything to keep it and he began to hate himself for what he'd become. Desertion that came in many forms, and—

And suddenly, he was there again, somewhere he didn't want to be. Nursing a bad case of jet lag while his ulcer churned around two months' worth of junk food and catered hors d'oeuvres. Schmoozing with those who went by the name of Clout when all he wanted was a meal with a wife who didn't answer the phone though he'd been calling at all hours. Lying awake through another sleepless night in yet another maid-service-clean room in some town just like the one he'd left behind a day before.

Home at last in L.A. Hearing a shriek from his bedroom. *Christine!* Racing up the stairs of the mansion, fearing his wife was being raped—or worse.

It was worse. He saw his life clearly in the picture of two sweaty bodies thrashing on his bed. Later Christine would say that she'd screwed the record company's head honcho to boost Neil's career. And she did so enjoy the benefits she'd earned for herself, even if she did have to put up with a husband who hadn't been changed by fame, who still talked like a poor boy reared by bayou folks.

He watched them climax, then shut the door. Softly.

"Neil? Neil, I asked you a question. Why would I be so cruel as to set you up when you were trying to protect me?"

"You tell me," he demanded, trying to forget what could never be forgotten. "Why would any woman?" Then, wondering if Andrea had some answer he hadn't been able to find, he shook her, then stopped, afraid he wouldn't be able to quit. "*Tell me.*"

"I can't. I can't understand any woman turning on a man like that."

"You're sure?" Still unconvinced, he persisted. "Sure you wouldn't cram some humble pie into my mouth to watch me gag?"

"For God's sake, Neil, how could you think me capable of such a thing? I've eaten enough humble pie in my life to know it's not pleasant. I don't have to shove it down someone else's throat to make a point." She said it in that peculiar streetwise but untouched way she spoke sometimes.

"The truth is," she said gently, "I fully intended to let you walk me home. I just wanted you to 'fess up' first. You play hardball. Consider it a rookie's attempt to take on a pro."

Damn her. Damn her for reducing him to all but begging for the honor of walking her home when it was a given all along. Christine had done a real number on him, but even she hadn't messed up his ability to create. This tough little number had a hold on him as no woman ever had before, not even his ex.

Dangerous. The woman was more dangerous than the queen in a bevy of killer bees roosting on his too-willing person.

"Make you a deal, Hot Lips—if I may be so bold as to call you that, since you've made a believer out of me. I'll dance with you in the dark, *if* you'll walk me home."

Six

"Do I get a good-night kiss, or even better, one right now to seal the bargain?"

The brush of her lips over his knocked out whatever sense was left in his brain.

"Consider it sealed." She wrapped an arm around his waist, while she stroked the tight cords of his neck with the other. And then he felt her fingers pull off the rubber band on his ponytail and sift through the hair he'd meant to get cut last month.

Maybe he'd wait a bit longer. The slight tug through his hair, the nails pressing into his scalp . . . Lordy, he was somewhere between heaven and hell but nowhere near purgatory. His own hands couldn't fill themselves fast enough. He caught the silky length of her hair, then wound it tightly on his hand. The tresses were the color of fire that all but scorched his fingers and heated up the rest of his body until he felt delirious with the fever.

He began to sway as the first strains of his frustrating brainchild escaped the lips he pressed against her temple.

"That was the lead-up," he confided. "Harmonica backed by bass guitar, and just a hint of a synthesizer tabbed on the sound of wind. A stormy wind."

"I love it. What's next?"

He didn't want to consider just why he was so thrilled that she, too, was swept up into the magic he'd long quit trying to understand.

"Do you feel me against you, hard and hurting and alone?"

"Yes," she whispered.

"Then tell me if you can hear it with this." He made sounds that passed for a saxophone, while in his ears he heard scat vocals and the trill of a piccolo. "Does it strike a chord inside you? Something so deep you feel it as much I do?"

"Yes. Yes!"

"Describe what you feel."

"I—I feel as if you're dipping me to the floor—"

"I am."

"But it's more than that." She clutched at his bent waist with an urgency that made him groan. "It's as if . . . I want to pull you down with me, but the anticipation's too good to give up and I'm fighting myself because I never want the want to end."

She didn't fight him as he slowly raised her, then locked her flush against him with palms sliding over the swell of her buttocks. The feel of her flesh through the silky pants was intoxicating, and it sent him diving into the heart of the melody that had eluded him thus far.

Now it burst forth with blinding light and sure power, expressing sorrow and ecstasy, tears and laughter. The tune told a story—their story. A lover's ballad without lyrics. Words never had been his forte.

He hadn't expected the finale, though. A swinging duet of alto sax interspersed with a . . . *harp*? Where the hell had that come from? Harps had no business with horns crooning jazz.

He didn't get it. Even after repeating it again and again while they flowed round the room as if they'd been dance partners all their lives.

Giving up, Neil hummed it one last time and took her down, dipping her low, then lower still. The small of her back fit neatly against his bent knee, while his other knee, against the floor, supported them.

The final strains left his lips on a whisper. He felt her hair sweep past his hand and onto the ground. He stared down at her arched neck. So delicate. So pale it seemed to glimmer in the dark.

His mouth descended. The tip of his tongue darted into the hollow, then swirled around it before flattening against the pulse point. He heard the sound of her breathing, shallow and dry.

He eased his knee away until she lay beneath his braced arms, then quickly swung a leg over her thighs and secured a mating position—all dominant male, hard and hunkered over a prone and soft female who was anything but soft inside. It was a familiar position, but the sensations it created were unfamiliar, bewitching. And threatening.

"I want to kiss you." He said it like an accusation.

"*Just* a kiss?" she asked.

"No."

"I didn't think so." A week ago he'd made her ache for more than a kiss. She still did. But now she ached for something else as well. She, with a foolish heart, was falling for this dark knight in tarnished armor, and disregarding the danger he clearly posed. But perhaps she posed a danger to him too. The odds weren't so scary when they were even.

"Is there a chance you'd be willing to settle for just a kiss?" She held her breath and waited.

He lowered his body to hers, and the hard male part of him nuzzled her closed legs, which begged to open for him, only for him. His powerful chest covered her breasts, which tingled and hurt with the need to be taken into the mouth that hovered over hers.

"Would I settle for just a kiss?" he repeated. "I would. And I will. Beggars can't be choosers, and I need to kiss you so bad, I'd even beg for that. Never begged a woman for nothing before. I can't work, Andrea. Can't sleep any better. Does that make you happy, since you didn't stick me with pins to cause insomnia or creative block?"

His unexpected answer was more arousing than the gripping need to feel him inside. Andrea wet her dry lips . . . and connected with his, they were that close.

"I'm sorry for that. But I'm not sorry that I'm on your mind and—"

"Under my skin."

"Am I?"

"Like a splinter to the bone. Gloating yet?"

As much as she should be, since it did give her the edge, she wasn't. Her purpose was changing with each of their encounters, until she wasn't even certain anymore what it was.

"Here's a news flash, Neil. It's pretty hard for me to gloat when *beignets* lose their flavor and I've been using triple coats of concealer to hide the circles under my eyes." She laughed softly, but her voice caught when he slid a hand over the swell of her breast. "At least I'm fitting into my jeans again and—"

"And since we seem to be feeling much of the same, can I hope for a change of heart? Exercise is one thing—although our exercise could be very enjoyable—but I'd much prefer to see you to safer and closer quarters. I was wrong to be such a jackass before, but you're wrong to let your pride get in the way of good sense."

"Back to that." She sighed. "I thought you'd gotten the message, Neil. Put yourself in my position—"

"You mean . . . like this?" In one smooth roll he had her on top of him, her hair a canopy over their faces. He took a long strand and traced her lips with it. "I like it both ways. How about you?"

"You're trying to manipulate me."

"Of course I am. And wouldn't you be just a tad disappointed if I didn't care enough to try to sway your mind to our mutual advantage?"

Andrea frowned as she considered his question. Her frown deepened with the silent acknowledgment that his blatant scheming gave her a thrill of feminine power. And yet he held the greater power, because deep inside she was still a small girl who prayed every night that someone, somewhere, would want her, funny teeth and all.

She'd tried so hard to be the best at whatever she did, to prove she was worthy of being wanted. It made her a little sick to think of how desperate she'd been to please, her need for affection blinding her to an old man's fumbling touches. Her words against his in front of a judge who turned out to be his golfing partner. Good-bye, Ivy League. Hello, community college, thanks to the state grant and job cleaning tables in the school cafeteria.

She'd learned the hard way to protect herself from being a victim of others' self-serving interests. She couldn't forget that Neil's interests, though sincere and caring, were self-serving too. He wanted her, but not for the reasons she craved: a relationship worth building on, a home like one she'd never had that was full of shared joys and sorrows, standing shoulder-to-shoulder against an unkind world.

At least Neil had been honest. He deserved as much from her.

"If you really want to put yourself in my position, Neil, then try to understand where I come from. It does something to a person to live on handouts most of her life—"

"I did it," he said, resentment and empathy in his voice.

"Then maybe you can understand why I'm driven to make it on my own. There's nothing like poverty to fuel ambition."

"And nothing like ambition can guarantee poverty

of a different sort. Best be careful what you ask for, 'cause you just might get it. Believe me, the having's usually not near as good as the imagining. You don't ever stop paying those dues."

"Then why do you have such a problem with me paying mine? I know better than to think it's your altruistic nature making you so concerned about my well-being. There are plenty of willing women out there. So why me? Is it the challenge of pursuing the unattainable? That's ambitious, you know."

He twined her hair about his finger and gave a quick, hard tug that brought her mouth down to a whisper from his.

"So you think you've got me all figured out."

"Don't I?"

"You're applying to me some lesson you learned from somebody else. Who was he?"

"Let's just say he was a good teacher, and I always learned fast."

"Then learn from this—you're right, there's not an altruistic bone in my body. But you're wrong about most everything else. I want more from you than some piddly-ass chase so I can preen once I've had my way and sent you on yours."

"Then what do you really want from me?"

"I'm not sure yet. I want you in bed, but not until you invite me there. Why, I don't know either, because it's a first for me. You've got something I need. Besides that, you're driving me so crazy, I'm offering you an even crazier deal. Let me set you up. Two keys, and you keep both until you decide to share."

"But you already said the having's not half as good as the imagining. Aren't you afraid of being disappointed?"

"I'm hoping I will be. And hoping I won't. I've never met a woman like you. A woman I wish I could take home to Mama and then make it with in the backseat of a car."

"I have a confession to make," she said, wondering

why she was freely giving him more leverage than he already had. "You see, Neil, for some reason the men I've known have never wanted to take me home. They just wanted to make it with me in the backseat of a car. Or at some out-of-the-way place, away from a wife I heard about from someone else in time to cancel the next date."

"Jerks," he muttered, then added angrily, "you're not that kind of gal. If I had a mama, I'd take you to meet her. And *then* put the move on. Heavy-duty."

For a full minute she said nothing, too elated to question if this was no more than a line, a means to get what he wanted.

A line. A byline. Then she realized her need to know him had nothing to do with a story, and everything to do with her heart. Why couldn't anyone trace his mother? He'd probably paid plenty to see to that, but why? He'd been quoted as crediting her for his love of music, but more than that he wouldn't say. Would he tell her, Andrea, share with her what he refused to all others?

"Has your mother passed away?" she asked gently.

"Dead," he bit out. "Died young and left me behind with a father who said music was only for sissies, and he couldn't stomach sissies. Just tramps to screw while the bedroom door's open, and fellow welders to bet the week's paycheck against in a cock fight."

And she'd thought herself deprived. How she hurt for the boy, and for the man who'd learned too well to protect himself. Suddenly, she saw him as needing all the same things she did. Things that neither of them had ever had.

Could it be they might find them with each other?

"I'm sorry, Neil," she said compassionately. "I'm so sorry."

Why was he too quiet? And why did she feel him

shiver before he rolled himself back on top of her and sit right on her hips?

"Don't you dare pity me," he said in a gritty, unsteady voice. His rough fingers yanked open the mother-of-pearl snaps of her shirt. "Pity yourself, *chère*, for being the object of my current desire. I've never wanted a woman as bad as you, and I always get what I want."

Seven

Neil had one hell of a surprise. For such a little bit of a woman, she had an amazing amount of strength. His head was still spinning and he was still blinking when he found himself lying on his back, with her standing above him and her foot wedged between his legs.

"How'd you do that?" Neil demanded uneasily. He could hear the sound of her catching breaths while she rebuttoned her shirt.

"Jujitsu." She sniffled and that disturbed him more than the threat created by her foot. "*Four* semesters, Slick."

"Are you crying?"

"No."

"Good. I hate it when a woman cries."

"In that case, *yes*. Yes, I'm crying. And it's your fault. Proud of yourself?"

"Hell, no! I've been nicer to you than I ever thought about being to anyone else. Certainly nicer than you've been to me so far. Here I offer to put you up in style, no strings attached, and what do I get for that? A heel in my crotch. Now, just what the hell are you cryin' for?"

"You don't want to know."

"If I didn't want to know, I wouldn't have asked. Lay it on me. And while you're at it, I'd appreciate you putting your foot elsewhere. I prefer to suck toes minus the leather. Please keep that in mind for future reference."

"How cocky can you get?" she managed between sobs.

"If you put on any more pressure with that foot, there's not gonna be one worth crowing about." He heard a small hiccup and an even smaller chuckle before she spun around and ran to the door. It banged shut just as he got to his feet.

"Andrea! Andrea, get yourself back here." He threw open the door and stared at the empty hallway. Hearing the rapid clicking of her heels over hardwood floor, he followed. "We've got some business to settle, and—ah hell, just don't expect me to grovel and ask your understanding for something I don't understand myself."

By the time he was outside the bar, all he could see was a jostling crowd swallowing up a flash of red hair in the distance. With a curse he locked up and took off after her, never more thankful that he stood taller than most. He quickened his pace, dodging the stream of partiers.

Andrea ducked past a sleazy barker and into a novelty shop. Neil was winded by the time he saw her crouched down in front of a souvenir display. He picked up a T-shirt off the rack near her hiding place and dangled it in front of her face.

"Sure you wouldn't rather have one of these? My treat."

"'Shuck Me, Suck Me, Eat Me Raw'?" she said in those snooty clipped accents of hers, apparently unimpressed with his peace offering. The garment showed a crawdad and tips on how to eat it.

"I like 'em better cooked myself." He dropped the T-shirt into her lap, meaning for her to have it whether she wanted it or not. "Tell you what, Lou's got a shrimp and crawdad boil planned next Sunday. I've got a sub sitting in onstage, so why not take off the day and come with me? I'll teach you how to eat a crawdad. Be nice, and I'll even feed you a few. Not only that, I won't dock your wage. I'm willing to pay you to keep me company."

"No thank you for the invitation and no thank you for the shirt." She flung it up at him, and he caught it in the face.

When he glowered down at her, she stood and fixed her gaze on an array of porcelain dolls. After studying them too intently, she carefully took one from its stand. Dressed as a court jester in purple velvet and gold satin, the delicate Harlequin figure coaxed a wistful smile from her. Neil fought the urge to snatch the doll away and demand she smile for him instead. Good God, what had this woman done to him? Actually reducing him to a jealous fit over a doll, when Christine's betrayal had only summoned his self-disgust for having married her.

"Go away, Neil," Andrea said evenly. "I can see myself home. We're through talking for the night."

"Apparently, you *can* see yourself home. But we're not through talking by a long shot. What's eating you?"

"You, that's what, and—"

"You folks need any help?" the shop clerk asked. "We close in five minutes."

"How much for the doll?" Andrea's polite tone, the one she used with everyone but him, made him madder—and he was already chewing nails.

"Sixty dollars. But I'll make it fifty for you."

"Will that price still be good next week?"

The man looked from her to the doll she gently stroked. "I'll give you two weeks, how's that?"

As Neil watched her reluctantly replace it on the shelf, he felt his anger cool. The urge to buy every dumb doll in the place for her was strong, but she'd already thrown one present back in his face. He didn't care to get pelted by a slew of flying porcelain.

Andrea expressed her thanks to the clerk, then brushed past Neil. He tossed the spurned T-shirt to the man and muttered, "Hang on to that doll. I'll be back for it tomorrow."

She didn't get far before he gripped her arm and spun her around to face him. Her cat-green eyes all but hissed up at him where they stood in the middle of the blocked-off street.

"I've got my beef, and you've got yours," he stated bluntly. "Only you know what mine is, and I'm still waiting to hear yours. Spit it out."

If there was anything she wanted to spit out, it was him. Spit him out of her system and fulfill her original mission.

"I reached out to you, Neil, offered my understanding. But you're afraid to let anyone get too close, aren't you? It threatens you. So what do you do? You reduce everything to money and power plays. You're a control monster, that's what you are. Well, you don't control me, buster. No ones does."

"And that doesn't make you a control monster too? Like recognizes like. Two peas in a pod, if you ask me."

"I'm not asking you," she said defensively. "But I am *telling* you something. If you ever try to manhandle me like that again, you'll be singing soprano permanently. Got it?"

"You mean you don't like it too frisky in the boudoir?"

"*See?* You're doing it again! No wonder your wife said all those horrible things about you." Her voice faltered as his eyes squinted meanly and his face turned ominously dark. Still, she plunged on. "A smart man knows that the quickest way to a woman's bed is through her heart and mind. Please keep that fact in mind for future reference," she added, imitating his drawl.

He muttered something that sounded like "the

Vow" before he looked away. Then, as if drawn back against his will, he looked her full in the face and tightened his grip.

"I know the facts just fine, thank you, ma'am. Now I've got a few for you. It just so happens my *ex*-wife taught me to stay out of a woman's head and never get near her heart, 'cause a man could lose himself in there. And once he does, he's left wide open for a she-cat attack—not to mention her taking a swipe out of his bankroll."

Andrea didn't want to soften inside, but she did. She wanted to wrap herself around him and beg him to let her undo the damage another woman had done. Instead, she stared mutely into his now-cold eyes.

Taking a deep breath, she touched his cheek and felt him jerk. As she stroked, he subtly relaxed.

"I shouldn't have said that about your ex-wife. That was a low blow and totally inexcusable. For her to have hurt you so deeply . . . well, you must have loved her very much."

"No love lost between strangers, *chère.* Kids make stupid mistakes, and Christine was one of my bigger ones. Much as I like to put all the blame on her, I can't. She dangled the bait, and I swallowed it. Found out too late that lust and love are two different animals. At least, I hope so. Never been in love, so I can't say fo' sho'." He shook his head and laughed that grainy sandpaper sound that stirred her on some primal level. "Listen to me. You'd think travelin' the world would've taught me some proper diction. I try real hard, but my roots won't let loose."

She felt as if he'd let her in, through a secret passage that led to a vulnerable part of him she never would have guessed existed. Before he could shut the door, she seized the opportunity.

"I like how you talk. I guess you could say I feel about it the same way you feel about my teeth. I can't change them, and I've always hated them because they weren't perfect. But after you kissed me, I didn't mind my spaces at all. I wish you felt that way about your speech. It's special. Like you."

"Hmmm. Never thought about it in *them there* terms." He smiled crookedly. Then, as if in a hurry to say what he wouldn't if he paused, he added quickly, "Christine hated how I talked. Said to keep my mouth on my sax so I wouldn't embarrass her by opening it. 'Course, I only talked louder and cruder then, just to make her mad. We were married six years, but it seemed like sixty. Hell had nothin' on her. Or me."

Andrea had never met Christine, but she neverthe-less despised her. Not only for putting Neil down, but for sharing six years of his life.

"Will you tell me about her?" Andrea hesitated. She wasn't a quitter or a coward. Neither had she been much of a gambler before taking the train to New Orleans. But what did she have to lose by going double or nothing? "And about your mother?"

Neil looked her over as he appeared to weigh his answer. "If you really want to know, you'll have to catch me in a weaker moment. Could make for some interesting pillow talk, I suppose. That is, should I be foolish enough to get inside that pretty head of yours. Oh yes, and you did mention something else about a heart. Best I give some thought as to whether getting you into bed's worth all that."

His deft fingertips slid up her spine and lifted her hair to expose the dampness of her neck to a muggy breeze.

Andrea traced the two-day stubble of beard shad-owing his jaw. "If you're feeling dangerous, why not sneak a peek into my mind right now? Tell me what I'm thinking, and you just might make it to first base after a string of strikeouts."

His lips pursed into a pout, then formed a sly smile.

"Why, Andrea, I do believe you've reconsidered my

invitation to Lou's party. What-say I pick you up around one on Sunday? Dress with a hot, laid-back afternoon in mind, and leave the table manners behind. Maybe we'll even do body shots and end the night with a kick."

"Body shots?" The way he'd said it promised a lethal sensuality.

"Don't tell me you haven't traded a few."

"I don't think so. Guns aren't involved, are they?"

"Not unless you count a bang." He laughed then, an indulgent, satisfied laugh. "Did I make it to first base or strike out again?"

"You could make it to second by not insulting me with another offer to pay me for being where I want to be."

"You mean Lou's party."

"Lou's party. Work. Wherever. I just want to be with you."

He regarded her for a full minute, his gaze somber. But then he quirked a brow. "So tell me, *chère*, does this mean I still have a snowball's chance in hell to score a home run?"

"You have to pass third base before you get there. You could up your chances by walking me home."

"But no frisky business, right?"

Her only answer was a smile.

They walked in companionable silence, his arm protectively about her shoulders. Hers moved from his lean waist to scratch his broad back as they climbed the stairs to her apartment.

"Nothing better than a good back scratch, *chère*. What's that about you scratch mine and I'll scratch yours?"

"Stop that, Neil!" She laughed uncontrollably when he rubbed two sets of knuckles up and down her spine before goosing her ribs. "I'm ticklish."

"You hate it. You love it. And then you laugh at the pain 'cause it hurts so good."

She hadn't understood the first time he'd said

that, but it clicked now as she giggled and struggled, then collapsed against his chest.

"What am I ever going to do with you, Neil? You are the most impossible, irresistible man I've ever met in my life."

"I'll tell you what you can do with me. Invite me inside, and let me make up for the last time I was here."

"I'm not going to bed with you."

"Certainly not. I meant it when I said I wanted you out of here, two keys for you and none for me till my fatal charms convince you to share. But since you don't seem of a mind to let me do that—*yet*—at least let me watch you take out the voodoo pins and fish my glossy out of the trash."

"I didn't trash it. Even if I did come close to burning it in effigy."

"Am I charred?"

"Just a little singed. Lucky for you that you came after me tonight and . . . apologized, sort of. The glossy thanks you."

He chuckled as she shook her purse to locate her keys. It was so dark in the hallway, she couldn't see to find them.

"Darn, I wish my landlord would replace the bulb. I left a message on his answering machine yesterday. If I had a ladder, I'd do it myself."

Neil's chuckle abruptly ceased, and she wished she hadn't brought up the subject. Feeling his disapproval in the taut silence, she was relieved to grab a hold of her keys.

"Can I come in?" His breath tickled her ear, and his chest brushed her back in a soft persuasion. "I promise to be good."

"Of course—" Had she put away her typewriter? She couldn't remember. Either it was stashed safely in her wardrobe or still sitting on the small table in clear view. "Of course not," she said, feeling frustrated and flustered.

"And why is that?" He leaned in closer, and she shoved the key into the lock, gripping it as if it could save her from something she really didn't want to be saved from.

"Because . . . because it's a mess, and you were less than impressed after I'd just cleaned. I'll say good night now and see you at work tomorrow, or make that later today."

She should be unlocking the door. *Why wasn't she unlocking the door?* Was it because his arms were wrapped around her waist and his palm softly rubbed a slow circle around her belly that quivered beneath his touch? Or maybe it was the touch of his lips nuzzling her neck and the trickle of Cajun French words she didn't need to understand to blush at them.

What power did this man have over her? She felt it with greater intensity each time he put hands on her. She was slipping, succumbing to a force that terrified and thrilled her.

"You're fighting me. Fighting yourself," he said quietly. "Don't. It's a no-win battle, *chère*."

"Don't—don't you need to write down your composition before you forget it?"

"I'll tell you a secret," he murmured. "I call my muse Simon. And Simon says remember. I always do. Right now all I want is to hold you, kiss you, and maybe even risk getting a bit closer to the heart I can almost hear racing in your chest. Can you feel mine?"

"Yes." She felt more, and it was that more she feared.

"But you're pulling away from me. How come?"

"It's the way you're touching me."

"But I've touched you before. We danced with my hands on your—"

"Please, Neil. Don't—"

"Mention how we kissed the first time, the way it ended? You remember, don't you? I got a little carried away, and my fingers went between your legs, while my palm—"

"Stop it," she groaned, frantically clutching the key because she didn't trust where her own hands might go once she released it. "I don't want to hear any more."

"Maybe because . . . you like hearing it too much?"

"Yes—no! I don't know. All I know is you're trying to seduce me, and I'm not ready for that. Not after tonight."

"Seduce you?" He laughed. "Believe me, *chère*, if I was bent on seducing you, our current position would be lots more intimate than this. I'd already have us on the other side of this door, with your back against it, those gorgeous legs wrapped round my waist and my pants on the floor with your panties."

His hand slid between her thighs, and the glide of his fingers was more than she could bear. She moaned low in her throat and slumped against the door.

"My, but you're hot, and so wet your pants are damp." He caressed her until she thrust against his rhythmic rotation. He slid his palm away and stroked her belly. "Seduce you? I could. But I won't. You mean more to me than that."

It was then she understood the danger she was in, the reason for her fear. *This* was intimacy. A gentle brush of palm to belly, a chest pressed to her back, and a man whose power lay in tender, nibbling kisses. *This* was a hold that could claim her soul. She wanted it so much, she dared not take it, because once she did, he might seize it back and destroy her dreams of having him this way. *This* side of Neil she could too easily love.

"You scare me, Neil. The way you are now, you scare me."

"How . . . odd." There was pleasure and puzzlement in his grainy voice. "Seems I do need to get into that head of yours. Try to find out why I don't scare you when I try, then manage to when that's not what I'm after. Forget seduction; I just need to hold you."

He turned her in his arms and pressed her head against his heart. She felt an impulse to beg him to stay, to take her away, anything so he wouldn't leave her side. Hungrily kissing his chest, she loved his strength that was tempered by gentleness, fearing it and yet compelled to confront her fear.

"Kiss me," she demanded.

"Just a kiss?"

"No," she answered truthfully. To hell with striking deals, and so what if he saw her typewriter? She'd explain it away somehow.

His mouth came down on hers. Softly. Longingly. The exquisite rubbing of lips induced her to open hers fully.

His tongue slipped in. Agile and anything but rough. While her own sought to dart and parry, his was strangely subdued, treating her mouth with care. She sucked it, wanting the fire, the force of passion his tenderness had stoked.

When she realized his fervor didn't match hers, that his hands coddled and stroked while she clenched and gripped, she slumped against him. "I don't understand."

"Me either. Did I ever tell you I knew I was in trouble the first time we met, and I could hardly think for wanting carnal knowledge of your teeth? I love them. They're beautiful. And so are you."

"I don't want to say good night, Neil. *Stay.* Please?"

"No." Neil disentangled her arms and stepped back. "Just a kiss, *chère.* Best we leave it at that for now. There's something going on here I find most unsettlin'." He stuck a cigarette between his lips and lit it with a match, the flame illuminating his face. His gaze, troubled and dark, caught hers before he snuffed the meager light. "Go on in, Andrea," he ordered more than suggested. "I've got some thinking to do, and every time I look at you, my good sense takes off on leave."

She didn't wish him sweet dreams as she went inside her apartment.

Neil saw the thin strip of light bleed between the closed door and warped floor. He heard her stifled growl of frustration, the sounds of a couch bed being yanked out, then squeaking before two shoes hit the door.

Thud, boom, went heels to wood. *Flip, flop*—went a heart he'd thought long dead. It was so rusty, it hurt to feel the erratic pounding.

Damn her, he silently cursed even as his lips curved into a grin and he whistled his way down the stairs. He was hurting, but Lord, if it didn't hurt so good.

Eight

The Vow. Neil repeated it aloud several times while he stared at Andrea's open balcony door from where he sat in his sleek red convertible.

He'd parked in front of her apartment five minutes ago, but hadn't killed the engine. He could still drive to a pay phone, cancel, and make his getaway. Lots of other women were sure to be at Lou's party—available women. Then again, the women who'd made themselves available lately had only made him want Andrea even more.

Why had he walked her home four nights running and left with only a few kisses when he could have shared her bed? And why had he spent an afternoon changing bulbs in graffiti-marked hallways, then hunted down her lazy landlord to buy the hovel so he could fix it up, since Andrea wouldn't move?

What the hell was the matter with him? He'd finally figured it out this morning and nearly lost his breakfast. He was afflicted with a deadly disease that had him buying dolls, shaving for a date, gargling with mouthwash instead of brandy, and right now chewing on a breath mint instead of smoking.

In an act of defiance Neil immediately lit up. He

almost choked on his second draw when a lilting husky voice called from overhead.

"Neil!" She waved excitedly, then blew him a kiss from the balcony.

And then he did choke—at the sight of creamy white legs in cutoffs and even creamier breasts straining to get out of a halter she had no business wearing to a party where there would be a bunch of men. He wouldn't even be able to enjoy himself if he had to spend the day making sure they kept their hands off her.

By the time he got his breath and started to yell that she needed to change her clothes, Andrea called out, "Stay where you are, and I'll be right down!" then rushed off.

His hands gripped and ungripped the leather-bound steering wheel in the stifling heat. When Andrea appeared, he got out of the car and held open the passenger door, just the way his mama had taught him a gentleman behaved. No honking horns for a lady, which Andrea definitely was. Even in the skimpy getup that had his blood boiling.

"You got it cut," she said, stepping in front of him and ruffling the hair he'd spent big bucks on to get styled just right. He self-consciously raked it back into place.

"I like it," she said. He didn't like the fact that her comment made him wish he'd cut it a lot sooner. "But I liked it the other way too. And here I thought we'd be twins today." She shook her head back and forth so that her ponytail swished.

"Get in," he growled. When her laughter trickled to a stop, he added grudgingly, "Please."

Neil was glad she kept her mouth shut until they hit the highway. Then the silence began to unnerve him. With only the whipping hot wind whistling past, he turned on the radio.

A quick glance at Andrea won him a sweet smile. She said nothing, but as he took an exit, and the convertible sashayed a few miles through a tunnel of gnarled oaks dripping moss, her hand brushed his knee. He saw her slide a tape into the player. Soon after, a familiar instrumental filled his ears.

Neil turned off on an isolated stretch of dirt road, stopped on a dime, and jabbed the "eject" button. No sooner had he done it than she jammed the tape back in.

Jab. Jam. Jab. Jam.

When she slapped his hand away from the tape that bore the title "Color Me Grey," he jerked her around to face him.

"Shut it off," he roared over the blaring music.

"I see you found your voice again," she yelled back. "I thought that would get your attention."

"Okay, you got it. Now what the hell's the big idea?"

"You tell me." She shook off his grip and turned down the volume. "I thought we were going to have a good time, Neil, but all you can do is sulk. Have you got a problem?"

"I've got a problem with this tape. Turn it off."

"But it's my favorite. Considering the album went platinum and won you a Grammy, it should be one of yours."

With a vicious twist Neil almost dislodged the volume control.

"That was really mature," she said quietly. The hurt look in her eyes got to him more than her put-down. "This date isn't starting out very well. Maybe you should take me back home . . . unless you want to tell me what's the deal?"

How could he tell her there were things in his past that cut so deep, he shuddered to remember? That certain songs, like certain smells, were time-machine triggers, and he didn't want to go back there. No more than he wanted to face the present and the emotions that were gutting his innards.

Andrea refused to let him ignore his past or escape

the present. The stroke of her hand over his was forcing him to confront both. He felt an absurd longing to run home to a mama who wasn't there. How could she have left the little boy who had never quit needing her, who still searched for her in the mist, because if he could find her, they could go home, and he could grow up without hunger, hate, and the hard rules that now ruled his life.

Neil forced himself to turn up the volume until the sound of his own music spilled from the speakers.

"Excuse me, Andrea, but I'm in need of a cigarette and a bit of space. Enjoy the tunes."

He cut the engine and got out. As much as he wanted to run screaming into the bordering woods, he opted to slouch against the hood and stare into the distance. He stuck a cigarette between his lips.

Two feminine fingers grabbed his cigarette and tossed it into the dirt.

"I want a kiss," Andrea said, her soft palms cupping his face. "And then I want an explanation."

"I said I wanted to be alone."

"Too bad, because I'm not leaving you alone."

"Back off, Andrea. Any kiss you get from me now won't be the kind you're asking for."

"Funny, I don't remember specifying what kind I wanted."

The sneer he turned on her met with a smile so foxy, he couldn't stand it. She proceeded to shatter his protective shell.

"You know, Neil, I've never been in love before, so I can't really be sure. But I have to wonder if what I feel for you is more than infatuation since I have the strangest urge to hug you to pieces. Even when you're looking at me as if you want to chew me up before spitting me out to hitchhike my way back home. A home my landlord told me someone bought with cash because he didn't want to waste time with a bank. It seems he plans to gut and remodel, beginning next week. Strange, but I'm the only tenant who hasn't been paid to leave. Do you know anything about this?"

"What's it to you if I do?"

"It's a lot to me, that's what. You've given me what I've never had, Neil—a reason to stay, a sense of security."

"*I* make *you* feel secure?" he said, unable to believe it though he wanted to more than anything.

"You do. I've had to make my own way, see myself home with no one worried about whether or not I get there in one piece. Your concern for my safety means more to me than the money you use as a smoke screen to show that you care. It's the only way you know how to say what you can't, isn't it?"

She was killing him by achingly sweet, painful inches.

"Not on your life. Money's not the only way I can show what I feel. Take off that thing that barely passes for a shirt, and I'll prove it." When she hesitated, he knew a grinding impatience to touch her, to have her trust him without the sway of passion. He needed proof that she spoke the truth. What's more, he had to find out for himself if he could give instead of take, protect while he left himself exposed. "Did you hear me? I said take it off."

"But—but here? And why do you want me to—"

"*Here. Now.* And the reason why is unless you do we're getting out of here before I say something real stupid—like tell you I think I might love you too."

The glow on her face as she slowly peeled off the wisp of cotton was delicious torture. His eyes descended from hers, which revealed a timidity laced with eagerness that was far removed from his experience. It turned him on. It scared him. Almost as much as what he'd had the brainlessness to admit.

He was a virgin again, staring dumbly at a pair of perfectly round breasts. Pretty pink nubs were haloed by brown circles the size of silver dollars.

At heart he was an exhibitionist. But this was for

his eyes only, and a quick scan assured him they were amply hidden on a dirt road cosseted by trees.

"Take off the shorts and anything underneath. No hurry, the slower the better. I do enjoy a suspenseful show."

"But, Neil, I—" Her come-hither-and-touch confidence faltered. Her crossed arms blocked the view he couldn't take his eyes off of or get his hands on soon enough.

"Need some help?" In a flash his tank top was gone. "It would certainly be my honor to take off what little you've got left. And mine along with it." He'd said what he shouldn't have, but he wasn't about to waste the benefits of his confession. "After all, people who think they love each other just might be able to find out for sure once they get rid of anything that's keeping them apart."

She started to put her halter back on, her breasts bobbing and swaying.

"We'll be late," she said.

Neil frowned. Andrea wasn't a tease. And she'd made it plain several times in the last few days that she wanted a lot more than kisses. So why this? He aimed to find out.

Wresting the halter from her grip, he tossed it to the ground like a gauntlet. When she lunged to get it back, he grabbed her wrists and pinned her on the hood that had cooled down enough so he was sure she wouldn't be burned.

He burned. She was frying his insides to a crisp, and he was making certain that by the time they left, her own would be in no better condition.

"I think I love you, Andrea. But I don't have to think twice about skipping Lou's party to make love to a woman who doesn't screw, who I care for so deeply that I couldn't screw her if I tried. What's holding you back? You ain't a party animal any more than I'm a monk, and I don't get this."

Their sweat mingled as he rolled his chest over hers, over the sweet mounds he craved to touch, to suck. This he told her outright. And then she did that thing that made him crazy. She turned a shade of red and gave him a shy look of pleasure.

That look caused him to bring her wrists to his lips and kiss the imprint of his fingers. And that kiss bound her to him more surely than force ever could.

As she stroked his clean-shaven jaw, and then his windblown hair, Andrea's heart turned over. Somewhere between the removal of her halter and his aggressive pounce, she'd realized that loving Neil wasn't a possibility, it was a certainty. So why had she stalled the inevitable?

They were playing a whole new ball game, that's why. This wasn't a hot encounter in a roach-infested kitchen. This wasn't about needing to be wanted and wanting a dangerously tender part of Neil so desperately that she'd been ready to drag him into her bed.

No, this was something else entirely. This was love, the kind that came maybe once in a lifetime to the lucky. Something rare. Too rare to disregard the invisible roadblocks that wouldn't go away with the shedding of their clothes. She had to topple at least a few to get them to the final hurdle.

"I've got a blanket in the trunk," he said. "Whatsay I drag it out, and we lay it on the grass? And while you put aside any misgivings I don't understand, I'll give you plenty of reason to forget them for good."

"But, Neil, it's not that easy. There *are* things between us that might go away in a moment of passion, but they'll still be there when we forget to forget."

"Say again?"

"Well . . . for example, you didn't have to shave or cut your hair for me."

"Wish you'd said so sooner."

"That's what I mean. I don't want you to change, unless it's something you decide for yourself. Otherwise it's a quick fix, and those usually don't stick, because the reasons are all wrong. You've changed in a very short time, and so have I. Are we really falling in love? Or are we just falling for distorted versions of each other instead of the real person inside?"

"I don't know what's real no more. But I can tell you this—for the first time in my life I've met a woman I can trust, can talk to and feel like she hears what I don't know how to say. You're tearin' me up while you make me feel the closest to whole I've ever been. It's damn scary, and there's a good chance I won't be able to make it for the goal I've set my sights on. That's as honest as I can get. Now you be honest with me. Where does this leave us besides half-naked on the hood of a car, with my own gears just about stripped from needing to peel off your shorts?"

Despite the heat, Andrea shivered. It was more than his graphic sensuality. More than the way he slowly rolled her nipple between finger and thumb until her hips rose to meet his.

It was about *honesty*. Being worthy of the trust he gave her when she knew his trust was given only to a few. If she were as honest as Neil, she'd tell him about the pile of pages hidden in her lingerie drawer. And if she told him, where would that leave them? He'd never trust her again. He'd turn his back and leave.

And he *would* leave. She was certain if he discovered she'd come to him under false pretenses, he'd accuse her of deceit, call her a cheat and a liar. He hated cheats and liars. They were on a par with journalists. He despised them, and that's what she was, what she'd always be—it was what she did best, and she loved her profession.

Loved it so much she was compelled to write the

story she'd come for. No one would see it, no one but her. It wasn't in her to betray him, and hell would freeze over before she'd publish the pages of insights that helped her to better understand him. "Neil Grey, Man or Myth" she'd titled the work that grew by the day. It was her tribute to Neil. If only his distrust of people in general and women in particular didn't run so long and deep, if only they had a history together that could compete . . .

Then she could tell him the truth, and he would believe her. Then he might even read her article, see himself through her eyes, and open his own to what he shut out.

Maybe when their new love was no longer new, they'd be able to make it over that final hurdle. If they had the real thing—and she believed they did—he would understand the reason for her deceit, get over his personal prejudices and respect her choice of careers.

But that was later, and this was now. And for now there was an immediate obstacle they had to overcome. One that had to do with hard thighs straddled over hers, large palms that caressed her breasts, and eyes that burned hotter than the high-noon sun. It beat through the trees and heated her hands as they clutched his broad, slick back.

"Andrea," he demanded, "answer me. Where does this leave us? Either tell me quick or tell me later. A *lot* later." At the feel of him hard and pulsing, the urgency of his frenzied movements, she frantically shook her head.

"*No.* No, Neil," she panted. "Not here. It can't be here."

"Give me a reason. A damn good reason. 'Cause as it is, I'm half out of my mind to get inside you so deep, you'll feel me where no man's ever been. You want it. You know you do. You want *me.* All of me. Say it."

"I—yes. Yes! I do want all of you. But I need you to want me. *All of me.* And that means not here. My place, where you didn't want me before. It *has* to be there, because if you really love me, it won't matter where we sleep as long as it's together. Love me, Neil. Love me enough to share my bedbug bed."

He stared at her hard while his ragged breaths fanned her face. His head fell forward, and a bead of sweat dripped from his brow onto her cheek. A crude profanity exploded from his lips, and she flinched, then cringed at the force of his fist smacking the hood.

"Can't do it." Neil pushed away and picked up her halter. He flung it in her direction and snapped, "Put that on. Put it on now. *Now!* You don't know what you're asking me. If you did, you couldn't love me and still ask it."

"I do love you, Neil." The halter shook in her hands as she put it on. He didn't watch the way he had when she'd taken it off. No, he turned his back to her, and she saw the nail marks across his skin.

She went to him, softly touching the traces of passion he'd called from her. He stiffened, and she pressed a kiss between his shoulder blades.

"I do love you, Neil. But I'm still asking. I need this from you."

"Get in the car," he said abruptly, and jerked away.

Andrea waited until her vision ceased to blur before she turned around. The passenger door was open, and she saw Neil slouched in the driver's seat, puffing on a cigarette. As soon as she got in, he gunned the engine.

She gripped the leather seat to keep from sliding into his lap as the tires hugged sharp curves. Neil stared stonily ahead. She didn't touch him. She didn't speak.

The weighty silence, the hostile energy that emanated from Neil, told her she'd done the right thing.

They needed time, and plenty of it, before he'd be ready to hear her past sins and to share whatever dark secrets drove him.

She also knew, with a sinking heart, that she might grow old before Neil could give her what she needed.

Nine

"What's eatin' at you, Slick? You been here two hours and you ain't sucked a crawdad head yet. Jest pulling off beer tops with them gnashin' teeth and hurting Liza's feelins by turning up yo' nose at her gumbo. This here's a sociable occasion, and you ain't had two words for nobody."

"Not hungry. There's yo' two words." Neil took a swig of the Dixie beer Liza always bought just for him. Cheap stuff he preferred over that fancy brew everyone else was drinking. Including his "date," who was busy talking to another man on the wharf. Neil was close to stomping on out there and turning this sociable affair into a two-fisted brawl.

"How about two other words? Woman trouble." Lou slapped his back, then hooted. "Laaawdy! You got yo'self a bad case of heartthrob blues. I *knew* it. You been acting real strange here lately, son, and all I can say is more power to her. 'Bout time some woman made yo' head spin and turned you around in the right direction."

"Shove it, Lou. Between you and Liza, I got enough of that talk years ago. Feeding me more of that junk about God-given gifts and living by the Golden Rule than all the red beans and rice in N'awlins."

When Lou's big grin thinned into a tight line, Neil wished he hadn't mouthed off. Here it came. Again.

"We took you in, boy. Picked you up off the streets, put you in clean clothes that fit and got you back in school. For all the good it did. You even worse now than you was at thirteen. Mean and mad at the world, not to mention God for taking yo' mama and leaving you with that sorry excuse for a daddy. Seems you inherited some of his ugliness, tho' me and Liza done our best to wash it out. Not that you got a stitch of gratitude for our efforts."

"That's not true, and you know it, Lou. I am grateful. For everything."

"Oh yeah? Well, words is cheap. Actions speak the loudest. And yours leave a lot to be desired. I took you to my gigs, made sure you met the right people who could get you somewhere, and taught you everything I knew till you was teachin' me. And what did you do? Hooked up with a gold digger who screwed you up so bad, all you think women be good for is to screw. The least you could've done was dump her without dumping the kind of career most folks, including me, would give their eyeteeth for. Good as throwing God's generosity back in His face and—"

"And it's a wonder He don't take my gift away to teach me a lesson." Neil finished Lou's speech verbatim. "How many times do I gotta explain that it's not fun and games at the top? They's a bunch of cutthroat, money-grubbing assholes. You think they care about the music? No sir. It's the bottom line of a ledger. That's the language they speak."

"You learned to speak that language jest fine, or so you said between dry heaves and diarrhea of the mouth when I drug you out of a fleabag motel and ditched yo' gun 'fore you could sober up. Finding you like that damn near broke my heart. Didn't you learn nothing from me and Liza? The world and them that be in it ain't never gonna be perfect, Slick. Grow up and accept that. And while you're at it, do what you can to make it a better place instead of making it worse the way you've made it yo' personal mission in life to see to."

"And just how do you suggest I do that?"

Lou got that crafty look on his face, the one Neil realized meant he'd played right into Lou's hands.

"Since you be askin' my advice for a change, I'll give it, no charge. Seems to me you got a chance to rewrite history. I see a good woman over there, looking like she's wishing you'd get your butt closer to hers. Judging from the way her butt's built, I cain't understand why you'd rather sit here and get yours gnawed on by me."

"What's the big idea talking about the way her butt's built? Liza wouldn't appreciate it, and I don't neither."

The flash of pearly white teeth between generous lips let him know he'd been suckered in.

"That a fact? Like I said, you been actin' real strange here lately. Never heard you talk like you got owner's rights to a woman some other man, with more smarts that you've shown since you got here, might take up in yo' absence. Why not make Liza feel better by asking her for two bowls of gumbo? And once you're done, get that old sax out from the room you ain't slept in for way too long. Liza washed the sheets this mawnin' in case you and your lady decided to stay the night."

"Forget that, Lou. She's got some fool idea that if I really love her, I'll sleep over at her place."

"Only a fool'd have to think twice about that."

"I ain't nobody's fool, and I got a set of rules to prove it. Where she lives, Lou, it's nasty, and I hate it. Just like going back over twenty years and living in the squalor I saw Mama die in. Cain't do it, even with the smell of Lysol and fresh paint instead of Daddy's vomit, Mama's dyin' breath, and a troupe of whores and cheap perfume taking her place."

"Sho' you can, if you love Andrea more than you do
your pride and hate for what cain't be changed. And
I do suspect that you do, or soon will. It'd be good for
you, Slick. Finding out for yo'self that it don't matter
where your head rests, so long as it's next to the right
person."

"You sound like Andrea."

"I'll take that as a compliment. She be good for
you, boy. Now be good to her, and just maybe you'll
be invitin' me and Liza to your home come next
summer. It's way past due. For us. But mostly for
you. Gawd's seen fit to give you a second chance.
Take it, and don't blow it this time around."

Lou grabbed the bottle of Dixie in Neil's hand, took
a long gulp, and gave it back to him. "Catch you
later, Slick? Maybe some the wiser if any of this sank
past that thick skull of yours."

"You know you love me, Lou."

"That I do, and only Gawd knows why."

Neil got up and embraced his Big Daddy before
slapping a high-five and striding toward the wharf.
"Lou, tell Liza her gumbo's the best in all of Louisi-
ana if it's half as good as the last batch, and I'd like
two bowls, thank you. And as for my old bed, I'm
sleeping elsewhere tonight."

From the corner of her eye Andrea saw Neil step
onto the pier. She gripped her bottle tighter and
made some innocuous comment to the man standing beside her. She'd already sent several others on
their way. But Neil didn't know that, and she wasn't
inclined to tell him after their latest contest of wills
and his subsequent silent treatment.

An icy glass was pressed between her shoulder
blades. When she ignored it and the yank on her
ponytail, Neil slid his hand around her waist and
placed his legs on either side of hers. The posture
was unmistakably of a male staking his territory.

WIN THE ROMANTIC VACATION OF A LIFETIME...
PLUS $5000 SPENDING MONEY!

Take your pick — Hawaii, Europe or the Caribbean — and enjoy 14 passion-filled days and sultry nights if you're the winner of the Winners Classic Sweepstakes presented by Loveswept. It's *free* to enter, so don't miss out!

YOU COULD WIN YOUR DREAM TRIP!

Just peel off the FREE ENTRY side of our bright red heart, and place it on the Entry Form to the right. But don't stop there!

...AND GET LOVESWEPT EVERY MONTH!

Use the FREE BOOKS sticker and you'll get your first shipment of 6 Loveswept Romance books absolutely free! PLUS, we'll sign you up for the most romantic book service in the world! About once a month you get 6 new Loveswept novels. You always get 15 days to examine the books, and if you decide to keep them, you'll get 6 books for the price of 5! Be the first to thrill to these new stories. Your Loveswept books will always arrive before they're available in any store. There's no minimum. You can cancel at anytime by simply writing "cancel" on your invoice and returning the books to us. We'll pay the postage. So try the Loveswept romantic book service today!

Get a FREE lighted makeup case and 6 free Loveswept books!

Open the tortoise-shell finish case and the mirror lights up! Comes with a choice of brushes for lips, eyes and cheek blusher.

BOTH GIFTS ARE YOURS TO KEEP NO MATTER WHAT!

DON'T HOLD BACK!

No obligation! No purchase necessary! Enter our Sweepstakes for a chance to win!

FREE! Get your first shipment of 6 Loveswept books *and* a lighted makeup case as a free gift.

Save money! Become a member and about once a month you get 6 books for the price of 5! Return any shipment you don't want.

Be the first! You'll always receive your Loveswept books before they are available in stores. You'll be the first to thrill to these exciting new stories.

WINNERS CLASSIC SWEEPSTAKES
Entry Form

YES! I want to see where passion will lead me!

Place
FREE
ENTRY
Sticker
Here

Place
FREE
BOOKS
Sticker
Here

Enter me in the sweepstakes! I have placed my FREE ENTRY sticker on the heart.

Send me six *free* Loveswept novels *and* my *free* lighted makeup case! I have placed my FREE BOOKS sticker on the heart.

Mend a broken heart. Use both stickers to get the most from this special offer!

61234

NAME_____

ADDRESS_____ APT _____

CITY_____

STATE_____ ZIP_____

Loveswept's Heartfelt Promise to You!

There's no purchase necessary to enter the sweepstakes. There is no obligation to buy when you send for your free books and lighted makeup case. You may preview each new shipment for 15 days free. If you decide against it, simply return the shipment within 15 days and owe nothing. If you keep them, pay only $2.25 per book — a savings of 54¢ per book (plus postage, handling, and sales tax in NY and Canada.)

Prices subject to change. Orders subject to approval.

See complete sweepstakes rules at the back of this book. **LS1**

Give in to love and see where passion leads you!
Enter the Winners Classic Sweepstakes and
send for your FREE lighted makeup case and
6 FREE Loveswept books today!

(See details inside.)

Her latest companion stepped back. "This lady ith you, Neil?"

"Uh-huh." Neil's other hand, which held the bottle, ame around to pull her closer against him. He ressed the cold bottle between her breasts, and she asped less from the chill than from his action.

"Sorry, I didn't know."

Andrea bit back the retort that she didn't know it ther, since he'd been ignoring her.

"Now you do." The arm he'd all but wrapped round her tightened, and she felt the urge to throw im over her shoulder into the muddy bayou. "What's at I hear? Sounds like your name, don't it? I do elieve you're being paged from one of those picnic ables. Best that you trot down the wharf and go heck it out."

"Good idea, Neil. Nice meeting you, Andrea. Later."

"I don't think so," Neil said flatly.

"Uh . . . right. Enjoy the view."

"I am." Neil's chuckle as the third party took off nd fast became a low whistle. "And what a view it is. ll that creamy skin dipping and swelling's worth a ay-per-view showing. For an audience of one. *Me.*"

"You're sweating on me, Neil." She tried to sound ut out, but it was awfully hard when the feel of his hest against her back was sexy as hell.

"You don't like my sweat? I'm hurt, *chère.* Any-hing I can do to change your mind, since you eemed to like it just fine before I got into one of my nits?"

Did he have to sound as if he really meant that? nd did he have to roll the bottle between her breasts rhile his thumb swished close to her navel, spread-ng the trickle of condensed moisture over her skin ntil she shivered?

"I suppose there's a chance I could put up with it. fter all, I have been putting up with your—"

"Obnoxious, immature, and totally uncalled-for

behavior. I'm sorry, Andrea, and I mean that. I came to make peace and fetch you to come eat."

"And here I thought you came over to get rid of my latest company so I wouldn't have anyone to talk to."

"You could've kept talking to Liza or some of the other women instead of flirting with all the men."

"I wasn't flirting!"

"Don't matter. You're with me, and that's that. Please keep that in mind from here on out."

"Why? So you won't have to spoil Lou's party by straightening someone else out with a fist?"

"I ain't punched nobody out for a good five years, but if I caught someone laying a hand on you, wouldn't give a second's thought to it. Does that tell you anything?"

Andrea hid her smile behind the arm he'd crooked over her shoulder. "It tells me you've got a jealous streak."

"A mile wide and as far as the eye can see. Makes me feel very peculiar."

"And it makes me feel . . . wanted."

He dropped his arm. "Turn around. That's good. Now, look me in the eyeballs and get an earful of this: I want you. No deals and no strings. Here, there . . . uh . . ." He groaned.

"Neil?"

"Anywhere. Including your current residence, which is getting an overhaul whether or not you move out. There, I said it. And don't ask me to say it again, okay? I've got a jam session after we dig in, and hard as that was to get past the lips, they need some recovery time."

"Can I kiss them and make it better?"

"Can't think of a finer way to perfect my playing technique. You know, proper positioning of the mouth, correct fingering, tonguing and breathing just right."

With no more than the sultry stare he fixed on her mouth, a hot, liquid sensation pooled in her belly. Shaken by the intensity and quickness of her arousal,

Andrea pinched her legs together and tried to cool down by glancing away from the cause of her excitement.

He gaze connected with Lou's. He stood in a group close to the water's edge, but his attention was focused on her and the fingertip Neil glided over her lips. Even from the distance she saw Lou's big grin and the approving nod of his head.

"Lou's watching us, Neil."

"I just bet he is. Let's make this one worth watching. Give old Lou a thrill. Big Daddy thinks you be the best thing that's come along since buttered bread, where I'm concerned, anyway. Why don't you convince me that just maybe he's right, and quit worrying about who sees what?"

"Why don't I convince you elsewhere? I'm not comfortable with other people being privy to my personal exchanges."

"Me either. But these are my friends. Besides, you'll have to get used to it, keeping company with me. It's not near as bad as it used to be when strangers constantly came at me with cameras and nosy questions about my crazy life. Juicy copy for sure, but none of their business. Every now and then someone comes sniffing at my tracks again, so keep your lips buttoned—except to open them up for me. Do it now. I need a kiss. *Bad*."

"Neil, I—" Her mouth was silenced by his, while the bitter taste of guilt swilled around the tongue she couldn't force away from his to admit the truth.

And so she kissed him in apology, and with desperation that showed in the bite of her nails in his back. A low groan of delight was his response. Determination to nourish their love until it flourished and could stand up even to her deceit was in the hungry slant of her lips, the soft nibbling of his mouth's bottom lobe until he thrust his tongue deep and she fed upon it. She loved his earthy taste; she loved his rough edges and smooth moves.

"I do love you," she whispered urgently. "Love me back, Neil, until you don't think it's just a maybe."

"Put your mouth back here where it belongs, and don't take it away till I've made up my mind. It's gettin' close, real close. Being pissed in public's one thing, and I've got the record to prove it. But showing I care, in front of other folks, is not something I do. Kiss me. Kiss me hard. I want everyone to see what I feel for you."

She felt as if they were in a fishbowl, kissing like mad for anyone who wanted to watch. It wasn't a comfortable sensation, and yet knowing that his love of privacy bowed to the intensity of what they shared was heady. It humbled her. It amazed her.

She gave back as good as she got. For once she wasn't on the outside looking in, recording her observations of someone else's triumph or tragedy. Neil had had enough of both recorded in inky black on white against his will, and all because he couldn't stop himself from turning his pain into something moving and beautiful.

Was this how it felt to be in his place? To expose one's most intimate emotions because compulsion demanded it, regardless of the empathy or criticism or indifference of others?

Andrea tore her mouth from his and buried her head against his chest. It was horrible to be laid so bare. And just as wonderful to feel something so deeply that she didn't care what anyone else saw or thought because it was too stunning and grand to hide or compromise.

That mix of emotions captured how she felt about the growing number of pages in her drawer, pages she knew she should tear up to cover her secret. But just as Neil was driven to compose and perform, she was compelled to chronicle his complexity. Neil was in her blood, and writing about him was the only way to fulfill her need to understand him.

"You've kissed me plenty of times before, *chère*,

but you never kissed me like I was a raft and you were going under for the last count. If it was your purpose to sway a 'maybe' to a 'you betcha,' all I can say is, if I'm ever playing tug-of-war, I definitely want you on my side of the rope."

"Think we could leave early, Neil? Maybe after your jam session? I'm hanging on to that raft for dear life, because I'm close to drowning with no shore in sight."

"Lord, woman, let's get back to the party, then make tracks to our joint property." He squeezed her tight, and she squeezed him back until he picked her up in his arms and headed for land.

The sound of whistles and applause snapped her attention to the crowd raising bottles in a salute. Couples shared deep kisses not unlike their own.

But that wasn't what held her gaze and warmed her heart.

It was Lou dancing a jig with Liza.

Ten

"Care for another crawdad, *chère*?"

"I'm stuffed, but one more's too good to resist."

Neil tore off the head, cracked open the tiny lobsterlike shell with his fingers, and peeled off the strip of meat from its back. He teased her nose with the bristles on the head, and Andrea clamped her lips.

"Aw, c'mon, quit being such a priss. Suck just one head, and you'll beg for more. All the juices are in there. Tastiest stuff that delectable tongue of yours'll ever try." He darted a glance at his crotch. "Almost, anyway."

Andrea quickly reached for her beer, needing to wet her throat and avert her gaze.

"I sure like it when you turn that particular color. Can't help but wonder if you blush other places too."

"Quit it, Neil. Someone might hear."

"Yes ma'am, I do wonder about that," he said louder. "And I do look forward to finding out for myself."

"*Shh!*"

"Want me to shut up?" he whispered. "Then suck this crawdad head." When she hesitated, he raised his voice again. "Of course, any woman who can kiss like you, the only one I ever met who could match me, just might make me plumb forget to look and—"

"Give me the head," she demanded, snatching it from him. Shutting her eyes tightly, she put the head to her lips and sipped.

The spicy liquid wasn't bad. In fact, as long as she kept her eyes closed and didn't think about where the juice was coming from, she wouldn't mind another.

"Told ya," Neil said, chuckling. "Aren't you glad I went to the trouble of expanding your education?"

"Next time I'll thank you to go about it differently."

"Will do. Next lesson: body shots."

"Not here," she asserted.

"You don't even know what they are."

"I don't have to. There's a distinctly lustful sound about them. Kissing you in public is one thing, but that's as far as I'm willing to indulge you."

"And that's as far as I'd let anything go. My feelings for you, and those you claim for me, are special. Don't really know how to handle them, but they're between us and no one else. I was yanking your chain, hollering about the way you blush and such. As you well know, I covet my privacy. And if I didn't covet you, I never would've laid my mouth on yours that long and hot in public. Body shots, *chère*. Tonight. Alone. Best you make that your last beer."

"I've only had two."

"And I've only had one more than that. Least bit of drinking I've done in more years than you've been legal. Funny, but I've had the most fun today since I can't remember when. Lou's right. You *are* good for me." He kissed her and stealthily slipped his tongue inside. Smacking his lips, he asked hopefully, "And could it be that just maybe I'm good for you?"

She answered him by reaching into the pile of discarded crawdad heads that she'd repeatedly refused.

Putting one to her mouth, she kept her eyes on Neil as she sipped with an intimate smile.

"Jake, you have that licorice stick on ready?"

"Ready." Jake tapped his clarinet like a cigar.

The drummer twirled his sticks, while the players on slide trombone, harmonica, and violin warmed up. Lou wiggled his fingers, and Neil loosened the ligature on an alto sax, put in a reed—a thin piece of wood that the vibration of his breath controlled—and tightened the mouthpiece.

From her position on the sofa beside Liza, Andrea watched, enthralled with his adroit handling of the instrument. He worked efficiently, and yet with an affection that she hadn't seen him treat the one he used onstage.

"That's not the sax he usually plays," she said to Liza.

"Lawd, no." Liza kept her voice down to a whisper despite the cacophony of warm-up scales and the raised voices of twenty-plus guests crowded into the den.

"This here's the one Lou found him playing at Jackson Square for whatever change landed in his horn case. It's cheap and must have a million finger miles on it, but he can make it sound like a legion of singin' angels. I think he prefers it over the fancy brass that took its place. Maybe since his mama gave it to him when he wasn't much bigger than the sax."

"Did you know her?" Andrea leaned closer.

"Only what he told us. She'd already been dead a couple of years, but her memory goes deep for that boy. I don't think he ever forgave her for dying, like the poor woman had some choice in going someplace better than what she was living in. He's had a rough life, honey, and it shows. Much as he loves me, he'd tear my head off if he heard me spouting this out."

"I appreciate you confiding in me, Liza. Neil's not

very open about his past, and more than anything I wish I understood what makes him the way he is. My feelings for Neil are—they're special. More than special. Like him."

As she glanced to where he stood, their gazes met, warmly, then reluctantly parted when Lou called Neil to the piano.

"He obviously returns yo' feelings, honey. The air darn near hums when you two look at each other. That's why I told you what I did. There's a lot more to know, but better for that to come from him. He's like an old coon hound, protective and loyal to the end with those he trusts. But he can turn vicious on any hand who turns on him."

Liza's warning drove home to Andrea the potential wrath she courted with each strike of a typewriter key, no matter that what she was writing wasn't for public consumption. She'd have to work it out somehow, but for now, what she felt in this room was too good to taint with worry. This was Neil's family, and she was a part of it. No outsider looking in and longing to be wanted, she'd been welcomed, accepted, and embraced by their soulful laughter and warmhearted spirits.

The crowd grew quiet, and so did the other musicians as Lou played a ragtime. To Andrea's amazement, Neil put down his sax and joined him for a duet.

"You mean he plays piano too?" she asked Liza.

"That and I don't know how many other instruments, but he don't spread it around. He blew us away when Lou said 'Try this' on the piano one day and that boy picked it up like you wouldn't believe. Same with everything else that makes any kind of sound. 'Course, everybody knows what he does best. I imagine him knowing how to play most instruments makes it easier to put it on a score sheet. Ever see him do it?"

"Only work through one composition when he was

stuck." Remembering the magic of matching steps in the dark, she sighed dreamily. "But he didn't get around to writing it down."

"Well, if that ain't something, I don't know what is. No one gets a sneak preview, not even Lou. Next time get Neil to let you watch while he writes it down. It is some sight to behold. Kinda weird, even. His hand moving faster than an artist going crazy with a brush, and his eyes all glassy like they don't even belong to him but some demon inside that's taken over." Liza shuddered. "Almost gives me the willies."

The sound of shouts and applause broke into their confidential murmurs. And then Neil's "One. Two. Hit it" had the band sliding into a swing number.

Liza grabbed Andrea's hand and pulled her up. They bumped behinds, shimmied, and rocked and bebopped till they dropped. By then, most everyone else had do-wopped to the floor. Despite the air conditioner going full blast, the band members were wiping their brows and taking swigs from beer bottles. Except for Neil. He lifted a soda and toasted Andrea in silence.

Then his lips moved without speaking: *Body shots.* The promise of dangerous passion seemed to ring clearly over the crowd.

"If that don't beat all. Slick drinking a soda. My oh my, what have you done to that man? He usually has half a case of Dixie beer and most of a flask of brandy downed by this time of a party. Whatever spell it is you put on him, keep it up. And while you're at it, see if you cain't get his smoking down to a tolerable level. It's a miracle he can squeeze enough air from them lungs to blow a note."

"Last song," Neil yelled over the hubbub. A loud groan of protest went up, and he added, "Hang on to your pants. It's just me that's callin' it quits." At that, everyone groaned even louder. Neil grinned at Andrea and yelled for quiet.

"It's so nice to be appreciated that I'm leaving you

with something special. A new tune I wrote with a special lady in mind. Not all the instruments are here, but there's enough to get by." Pulling a sheet of paper from his pocket, he unfolded it and conferred briefly with the other musicians.

An excited murmur of anticipation swept the room, while Andrea strained to hear what he was saying. All she caught was "B flat . . . bring it in slow and easy . . . " and then snickers from the huddle at something that sounded like "harp."

"Cram it," Neil growled over the laughter. They got quiet fast, then Neil started chuckling. Startled looks passed between the musicians before they joined in.

"If I didn't see it with my own two eyes, I wouldn't believe it. Actually laughing at hisself instead of jumping all over folks for nothing. And dedicating a song to a woman?" Liza pressed her smooth brown hands together in prayer. "Glory be and hallelujah! I done seen a miracle."

"It seems a miracle is what it will take for him to ever perform for more than a packed audience at his club. It's a waste, Liza. The world should hear him play again."

"That it should, gal. Lou and me, we've said so to him till we're blue in the face. Maybe you can make him listen in time. Just be real careful how you go about it. He's funny about certain things, has these dumb rules I couldn't live with myself. Unless maybe . . . I was single and thirty years younger and needed him the way he needs you."

"I need him too, Liza," Andrea confessed.

"You must, to have stuck it out this far. He's hell on women. No use for 'em whatsoever, except for you know where?"

"I wouldn't know where, if that's what you're asking."

"I was, and that's all I needed to hear to tell you what he probably don't want to admit to himself after all his 'yickity-yack I won't have none of that.' He's of a mind to marry you. Finally found a nice gal to settle down with and make some babies. He'll be wanting a passel, do his best to keep you barefoot and pregnant at home. If you've got plans for some kind of career . . . well, don't say I didn't warn you."

Andrea couldn't believe what she was hearing. She shook her head, trying to clear it.

"I think it's too early to see that far into the future, Liza. We have the start of something wonderful, and I hope it's strong enough to last. But what you're talking about takes time. And where Neil's concerned, it could be a *lot* of time."

"When it's right, it's right, and time don't have nothing to do with love, except to test it, stretch it thin or make it grow. Mark my words, by summer's end you'll have a ring on yo' finger and a man on yo' hands with some *very* uncool ideas."

Andrea focused hard on Neil as he reached for his sax. Even with his hair cut and his face cleanly shaven she couldn't imagine him as Liza had depicted him.

"I can't see him like that. Maybe he has cleaned up his act some, but Neil wanting hearth and home and all that jazz? Really, Liza, that's too much."

"You don't want it to be true?"

"It's not that. Of course I want a home, a family of my own. I've never had one, and—"

"And neither has he, not the sort he's wanted all his life. Would you believe that *Father Knows Best* is his favorite show? Won't even switch the channel for *Star Trek*, and he's crazy for that nonsense. Before his mama took off to the sky, she fed him full of music, church, and a woman's place being in the home no matter how no-good the man was. It was that Christine and success messin' with his head that screwed him up again after me and Lou straightened him out. Now he's back on track and hot on yours, honey. Deep down Slick wants a *Father Knows Best* home. I just hope he don't get cold feet and end up sabotaging his chances like he did his career."

"You don't mean that he actually—"

The harmonica blew a mournful whistle, reminiscent of a train's lonely wail. The thrum of a bass guitar struck a minor chord. All conversation in the room ceased, including the two women's whispers.

The sound of a stormy wind, then the chug-a-lug of a train's steel wheels gathering speed rushed in from a vocalist, while a drum beat out the low roll of thunder that culminated in the crash of a cymbal.

And out of it emerged the sustained cry from a saxophone. His breath seemed endless, and his eyes fixed on hers.

Andrea was transfixed by the hold of his gaze, which dipped with his body as he swooped low and came up with a shower of raining notes, his fingers moving so fast she couldn't see more than a blur, couldn't hear more than a whisper of the trilling clarinet and scat vocals scaling octaves in a fanciful flight of pulsing emotion.

The drum beat on, matching the accelerating thud of her heart that was spinning out of control with each smooth step Neil took in her direction.

He didn't hold out a hand; both were on the brass he plied with stunning skill. But she felt his silent reaching out to her, felt drawn to rise from her seat and meet him with a sway of her hips, the placement of her hands on his waist amid the ripple of applause.

He arched back, never forsaking the mating of their gazes, and moved until his hard leg caressed her pale thigh and the brush of her lips to his bare arm caused his biceps to flex tighter. Kissing him there, softly, sweetly, while the swish-swish of flirting torsos elicited "ahhh's" from couples who drew closer until an orgy of saxophonic moans and hot whispers of promised kisses clinched the mood.

He wooed her with his gaze, his sinuous rub

promising a more intimate touch once they were alone, and she ached for his fingers to play her body in private with the sensitivity he played the crowd.

This was love. This was sex. This was everything in between, and it was beyond her wildest dreams because this was Neil at his best, seducing a cheap saxophone rich in memory with an inflection she'd never heard before. This was longing so deep it was desolate. Passion beyond an orgasmic cry. Need so poignant, he seemed to weep, *I want to go home, take me there and don't let me leave even if I head for the door.*

Her heart answered with a plea of, *Come home . . . yes, come home with me. I don't know where it is, but we can find it together. . . .*

All instruments were silent for Neil's run, a soaring cascade that ended with his lips departing from the mouthpiece—and falling on hers. The roll of his kiss carried her over the threshold of an emotional climax.

Before she could recover from the mad moment of lost control, he stepped back and thrust his saxophone at Liza, who was beaming.

Amid a standing ovation Neil called out, "Glad you liked it, 'cause I love the title. 'Andrea.'" With that, he hustled her out with his hand cradling her butt.

As they made for the front door, Andrea heard Liza's jubilant laughter, along with her lilting prophecy: "Forget summer's end. Make it two months, honey, and I don't mean maybe."

Eleven

"I'll get it." Neil put down the sack he'd kept hidden in the trunk until he'd parked his car in front of Andrea's apartment—which as of yesterday belonged to him. After tonight *she*'d belong to him too. He took the key from her unsteady grasp. "You've been awfully quiet since we left the party. Not to mention that your hands are almost as sweaty as they are shaky. What's bothering you?"

"I'm nervous. We both know why we're here, and it suddenly seems so deliberate. And—and I think you should know I'm not on the Pill. Is that a problem? Do you need to go to the store or—or I can go to the doctor tomorrow and—"

"For crying out loud, what has gotten into you? Get in here. We need to talk." He pushed open the door, grabbed the sack and Andrea along with it, then turned on the lights. Anticipation and anxiety rushed through his insides as he confronted the ghost of poverty past.

It was still a dump, and he didn't want to be here. But he wasn't leaving before taking his lady to bed and finding out how it felt to wake up next to her.

He clicked the lock and turned in time to see her chafing her arms as she warily eyed the couch.

"Well, are you gonna stare a hole through it or sit?"

"I'd rather stand. All that driving and—" She froze when he stroked her arm and leaned down to nuzzle her neck. "And it's hot in here. I'd better turn on the air conditioner." Breaking away, she trotted to the window unit. While she fiddled with knobs and vents, Neil frowned. He frowned even more when she darted from his questioning touch and headed for the kitchenette.

"I'm thirsty. Would you care for a drink?"

Grabbing her arm, he pulled her around to face him.

"No, I would not care for a drink. Not until you tell me what's put you in such a state. The way you're jabbering and jumping and just about as warm as a corpse—" The image caught and held, then released him with a startling quickness as he studied Andrea's distressed face. "Would you please tell me why you look like you're scared I'll yank off your clothes and jump on you without even bothering to pull out the couch?"

She glanced away, and he gripped her chin.

"Look at me," he demanded. "That's better. Now you answer me this. Did you take jujitsu for college credits, or did someone give you a reason to learn to protect yourself?"

She nodded stiffly, and he felt a stabbing pain in the region of his chest.

"I'm sorry, *chère*. How bad was it?"

"Bad enough for you to be the first man I've really trusted since. Bad enough to go to court and find out money and connections spoke louder than fairness and truth."

"Who was the son of a bitch?"

"A wealthy benefactor connected with the orphanage. He took an interest in me, set up a scholarship fund and made it clear I was to be the first recipient. I was grateful, especially since he didn't make me feel as though it were charity. It turned out he wanted a payback on his investment. When I refused, he accused me of leading him on. He pressed the issue, and I got away. But not before I thought I would never wash off the horrible, clammy feel of his old hands on me."

Neil had felt rage, hatred, before—he'd felt them so often, they were as much a bad habit as his vices. But he'd never felt anything like this. Grabbing her to him, he covered her with a fierce, protective embrace.

"I wish I could get my hands on him. By the time I got done, he'd be screaming to get his privates back. He wouldn't touch a woman again, not being a eunuch."

Andrea's soft laughter was a welcome tonic, soothing his furious boil down to a simmer. She was all pliable and warm again and making him want that something she had that he needed. Every time he held her, he got closer to it, and the closer he got, the more he was hooked.

"When you're through with him, do you think you could place a few warnings with some of the jerks I've had the misfortune to meet since? Don't ask me why, but I seem to attract that particular kind of man."

"Case in point. Here I be."

"You're not a jerk, Neil. Well . . . at least not always a jerk. You have many fine qualities."

"Such as?" He wondered if she counted ego. His wanted some strokes after all the mauling she'd given it.

"Let's see. You're a hard worker."

"I certainly am. The work ethic is alive and well in me."

"So is your attention to your person."

"Definitely. Even when I don't shave, I brush my teeth three times a day, take a shower twice, and wash my hair while I'm at it. Not to mention I wear only freshly laundered clothes. What else?"

"Um . . . you're talented, self-disciplined when it comes to your music, and you can be a lot of fun. You're honest, not a cheat or a quitter. Oh yes, and you're a marvelous dancer."

"That's all?"

"I'm sure there's more. Give me a minute to think."

That she had to think about it made him decide to help her along.

"For your information I'm also well read in science fiction. I can cook one mean mess of collard greens as well as jambalaya. Though I don't go to it, I contribute regularly to Liza's church. Furthermore, I like children, and it's mutual. You can even ask Lou. He's jealous because every time his grandkids come to visit, guess who they run to first? Me."

"Careful, Neil. You're starting to sound like *Father Knows Best*."

"My favorite show. *Star Trek*'s next. Shall I go on?"

"No! I'm convinced you have more than your share of redeeming virtues."

She laughed that bubbly sound he'd developed a mighty fondness for. It pleased him deeply that he'd made her happy again. It also pleased him that he'd had the opportunity to inform her of his more desirable attributes, which he figured made up for the not-so-desirable vices she was all too aware of.

He had more in both departments, but she'd learn about them soon enough. For now there was one quality in particular at the top of his priorities.

"I'll go on anyway." All play gone, his voice dipped low, and so did his mouth to tongue an earlobe. "I am also a wonderful lover."

"Lots of practice, right?"

"Lots of practice. But with all the wrong women. I'm ready to expand my résumé to include a nice gal."

"A nice gal, Neil, but one who probably falls short of your usual fare. I can kiss as long as you want, but beyond that, chances are I'll be a disappointment compared to the rest."

"You're the rest I've been waiting for. Listen up and get an earful of this: I'm glad you told me about what happened to you, because tonight I want to wipe it from your memory. I'll be slow and careful and as patient as I can be. If I do anything, say anything, that upsets you, tell me, and I'll make it right. Will you trust me to do that?"

"I do trust you, Neil. And I'm no less than amazed that you, of all people, proved to be the man who finally made me want to be touched again."

"Should I take that to mean that you haven't been with a man for more than a little while?" He slid a finger from her neck to her breast.

"I've had occasion to throw a few over my shoulder. As you said that night we cleaned up the bar, I wanted to keep kissing when some *monsieur* got antsy to move things along."

"It's a wonder you didn't throw me over your shoulder and out the door the first time I was here. Why didn't you?"

"Because for once *I* was antsy to move things along, and some *monsieur* wanted to keep kissing. And kissing. And kissing. My lips were swollen for two days. Every time I touched them, all I could remember was that kiss. Of course, it made me even angrier with you, and with myself, that I wanted more of your kisses. More of . . . more."

"Is that why you stuck me full of pins? You did take them out, didn't you? And where is that doll, anyhow?"

"That's why. Every one. And I threw the doll away."

"Hmmm . . . seems to me there was another doll you wanted."

"It's gone." For a moment she looked ten years old, crestfallen, her mouth turned down in pain over a broken dream. "My tips were extra good this week, and I went back yesterday. There were a lot of others, but they weren't the same."

"Close your eyes and stay put." Feeling like Santa, Neil went to his bag. There were lots of goodies in there, besides a doll.

"Neil? How much longer do I have to stay like this? And what's all that noise you're making?"

"You'll find out in a minute. Hold on to your horses and your britches while you're at it. I'm close to ready."

While she fought the urge not to peek, Andrea smiled. The noise he was making could have been the crinkling of gift wrap. Not that he hadn't given her priceless presents already. Compassion. Understanding. Making her feel wanted and making her want him more than ever because he'd put her at ease after her attack of nerves.

She heard the turntable rotating, a needle bumping, then grooving into a record before a scratchy feminine voice filled her ears.

"Billie Holiday," she said. "Next to you she's my favorite."

"Just so I come first. Open your eyes."

Andrea blinked. The room was dark except for the leaping flames of at least a dozen candles.

"I've got you something here," Neil murmured, his eyelids seductively drooping. "Hold out your hands."

He placed the doll in her waiting palms. Andrea stared at it for long moments, then hugged it tight against her.

"My doll! You bought my doll. Oh, Neil. Just when I think you can't turn me inside out any more than you already have, you do it. I love him. His name's Lancelot. I've got all sorts of names picked out for my kids, can you believe it? But Lance is my first. And it goes to him."

"How about that, our first child together, all dressed in velvet and satin, with silver bells dangling from his hat." He pinged one.

Had Liza actually pegged Neil right? Andrea wondered, staring from the doll's smiling face to the even bigger smile on his. Strangely enough, he looked like a big daddy, a very sexy big daddy.

"Thank you, Neil," she said faintly. "I love this doll, and every time I look at it, I'll think of you."

"I'd prefer you to do more than think. Give Lance another squeeze, then put him down. I'm in the mood for some body shots, and everything we need is ready."

Lance nearly got the stuffings squeezed out of him. He was soft and unthreatening . . . everything Neil suddenly wasn't.

He extricated Lance from her stranglehold and set the doll gently beside the couch, which he proceeded to pull out.

"I think you could use two body shots, *chère.* Maybe three, under the circumstances. Any more than that and this night's over before it gets started. Come the morning, neither of us is gonna be fuzzy and wondering what really went on. We're feeling what happens, wide awake. Starting with me watching you slip into something more comfortable before I slide off what's left. I want you easy in your skin."

"Are you asking me to strip?"

"Just your inhibitions, your fears, your past. Nothing I'm not willing to get rid of myself before we shuck off our clothes. Am I getting through to you?"

Body shots. Layers of clothes covering layers of what lay beneath. He was getting through, and she didn't need to find out what a body shot was to know what Neil wanted.

"You want more than my trust and more than my body."

"That's the general idea. Tell me what else you know."

"You're looking for something, and you think I've got it."

"You're batting a thousand so far. Let's take it further. What do you want from me in exchange?"

"I'm looking for something, and you seem to have it."

"Anything I've got is yours, *chère*. What say we make a fair trade? Starting with body shots. I'll go first, so you can see how it's done. Arch your neck."

Her stomach rolled over. Then rolled over again as his tongue forged a path of moistness on her neck. Then she felt tiny sprinkles raining down on the wetness.

"What's that?"

"Salt. And this is a wedge of lime. Hold the skin between your teeth so that mine can bite into the pulp once I swallow the shot."

Salt. Lime. The shot had to be . . . "Tequila?"

"Mezcal. Ready?"

Andrea nodded and placed the lime between her lips. Heat rushed through her when his head lowered and his tongue slowly lapped the salt.

Cool, humid air licked the wetness while he downed a jigger. Then his head lowered once more, and he bit into the pulp of the lime until he tugged it from her mouth. He replaced it with his tongue, a tongue that tasted of tart juice, the pungent bite of tequila, salt—and desire.

She felt woozy from his kiss, and she wanted it to never end.

It did. But in recompense he offered her the shaker of salt, as well as his neck. His knees bent, and one slid between hers. It moved insistently until her legs were spread and his hard thigh stroked the soft flesh at their juncture.

"I'll hold the shot for you," he said in a gritty whisper. "Lick my neck . . . good. More . . . harder. Ummm. Perfect. Sprinkle the salt on me and lick it till there's nothing left but your tongue and my skin."

She obeyed his arousing command and might

have forgone the tequila if he hadn't lifted her head by tugging on her ponytail.

He pressed the edge of the glass against her bottom lip, and she drank the liquid fire until it burned her throat and warmed her stomach. Tears stung her eyes as her teeth clamped down on the lime, and he fed her the fruit from his mouth.

He discarded the peel. He kissed her again, longer, deeper, a kiss that burned hotter than the liquor. His leg wasn't nice, not nice at all in the way it pressed harder against her, making her feel a keen discomfort there.

Again they traded necks. Again they took turns at the glass. A small trickle escaped to dribble down her chin. He sucked it into his mouth, and she threw down the jigger as well as the lime.

"I've had enough," she said breathlessly. "If you want another, you'll have to drink from the bottle and forget the lime. My hands belong elsewhere."

"The only thing I want is you." His finger hooked into the band cinching her ponytail. And then her hair was falling to her shoulders, and his fingers were thrusting between the strands. "I want you naked. I want your body loose and ready to take mine. And I want you to remember every word and stroke, every second of what we share. I want you to remember it for the rest of your life."

"That could be a lot to remember, Neil."

"Count on it. But don't worry . . . I'll make sure I give you a night you won't ever be able to forget."

Twelve

Neil knew one thing and one thing only. He needed to slip into her skin, listen to her heart, and climb into her head. All the way. He was taking this all the way, and he had to do it before the mist swallowed him, and he lost sight of what might be home.

He gripped her halter, his fists twisting into the fabric he wanted to rip off with the same urgency that had his stomach knotting and his arousal straining to get free.

"Slow and easy." He could only hope that by saying it, he could make himself obey.

"Yes. Slow and easy. I need that from you. And *this*. Making love here when I know it's hard for you. I wish I knew why, but I don't. Tell me when you're ready, and I'll be there to listen. To care. And I'll touch you as slow and easy as you're touching me now."

Her whisper commanded him. He pulled the halter over her head with a gentleness worthy of the trust she gave him.

This was heaven. It was hell. Wanting her with a fury, with the poisonous anger she diluted and slowly rid him of until he believed if he could spill what was left inside her, he'd be washed clean. Here.

n this room that took him back, back to the past he
shunned.

He closed his eyes against it, and her fingertips
raced his lashes.

"Neil? What's wrong?"

"Something's right for a change, that's what. I'm
not numb. Kept myself that way for years, with
booze, sex, music. Anything to ignore the stink of all
he garbage I've got piled up in me. This room brings
t all back and—and damn if I'm not selfish as ever.
Listen to me laying this on you when I should be
making you forget any man ever put a hand on you,
except for me."

"I'd rather forget together. Maybe the best way for
us to make bad memories go away is to share them.
I shared mine with you. I wish you'd do the same."

"They're not romantic, and this is a night for
romance."

"Now you're being selfish. And stubborn."

One thing about Andrea, he could always count on
her to say it straight and, as with castor oil, make
him thankful she had, once he had taken the dreaded
swallow. He took a deep breath and . . . swallowed.

"Okay, you asked for it. See, Andrea, I grew up and
saw my mama die in a place like this, and once she
died, I lived with worse. A lot worse. I lost my
virginity at twelve with a whore my old man brought
home and was done with. Wasn't that thoughtful of
him? A real father-and-son activity. I threw up after-
ward and never touched another prostitute since."

Even in the dark he could see her blanch. Would
she find him disgusting now? Had he blown his
chance in his rush to grab it and run? He felt as if he
were tied to a whipping post, and she could either
free him or lash him to the ground.

"How horrible for you, Neil." She pressed a deep
kiss into his palm, then laid her cheek there. So
smooth, so wet with the fall of her tears. "I hurt for
hat little boy. What happened to him after that?"

"He ran away, the way his mama should have bu
didn't. I take that back. She did, only she didn't tak
me with her." He wiped Andrea's tears, each dro
seeming to wash away another layer of accumulate
rot. Lord, but he was starting to feel clean. He love
her for this, for accepting him, purging him in a wa
no amount of money or prestige ever could.

"It wasn't ever good," he rushed on, eager to spi
the poison from his system. "Not with my old man'
gambling and drinking and slapping us around from
time to time. But Mama kinda kept it together. Sh
was a homebody. Always cooking, cleaning, trying t
take lemons and make lemonade. He didn't go com
pletely sour till she was gone. Guess you could say
went sour too. Learned to pickpocket better than
could play the sax. Got in lots of fights, and it's
miracle I didn't get my teeth busted out. Tha
would've put the skids on my career faster than I did
Lucky for me that Lou took me in. I owe him a lot
and my success is just a smidgen of it."

Andrea opened her mouth, then shut it. He ha
the feeling she wanted to ask him about his caree
but thought better of it. That meant a lot to him; fo
once a woman cared about him, the man, not th
man behind the music and the perks he coul
provide. It made him trust her that much more. H
could tell Andrea anything, and she'd keep his se
crets safe.

And because of that he'd tell her someday abou
his time on the road. He could entertain her fo
hours on end with the workings of the star-make
machine that had drained dry the creative urge and
fattened his pockets. A story full of tragedies and
triumphs that had twisted him till he resented hi
music—hated it.

The loss had been too much. Damn near took hi
sanity with it, sucking him to the bottom till he'
tried to destroy himself. Nope, hadn't been a cheat
ing gold-digger wife he'd wanted to die for losing. I

was the death of his art, the life squeezed from it by the industry's greed and his own blind ambition. He hadn't needed that gun to join his mama. Not really. Neil Grey, without his music, was already dead.

Great copy. An exclusive scoop. One he wouldn't share with anyone but her. And he would when the time was right.

This was *not* the time.

Neil looked around the apartment, then shifted his gaze back to Andrea. He smiled. Without a stitch of effort.

"Told you it wasn't very romantic. Did I kill the mood?"

"No. If anything, you made the night more intimate. You shared yourself with me in a deeper way than just your body."

Her hands glided sweetly over his chest, then tugged up his top. He got rid of it in a hurry. Threw it on the halter he was confiscating before the next party.

Neil rubbed his chest against hers, watching her nipples peek through his mat of hair, feeling the softness of her breasts create an exquisite friction before he cupped them in his hands and pressed them together.

He buried his face between them, listened to the pounding of her heart that called to his. No deceit there, no betrayal, no lies. The mist lifted, and he thought he saw home.

The sight of Neil's head pressed to her, feeling him nuzzle as he got as close as he could, all but tore her heart out. She held him tight, loving the texture of his hair sifting through her fingers. Hers. He was hers. At last, someone she belonged to belonged to her.

"I need to share my body with you." He kissed her palm, then slid it down his chest, past his navel.

He urged her fingers lower, lower, until she cupped him, her eyes wide. She was aroused as she'd never

been before. She was also more intimidated by hi:
abundant virility than she'd been by the horrid thin;
that had tried to push its way in and the gnarled
hands that had groped her before she got free.

This she told Neil, feeling a sense of wonder tha
she could say to him what she had trouble saying t
herself. As he nodded and murmured a soothin;
reassurance, her words flowed easily.

"Don't you worry, *chère.* Leave everything to me
First off, I think it would be a good idea for you t
confront your past enemy and discover a new all
who wants to pleasure you more than himself. Wh
not get friendly with him? Look. Touch. Shake hand
to your heart's content."

"Well . . . if you're sure you don't mind."

"Believe me, I *don't* mind. Oh, kissing's allowe
too."

"And you promise not to do anything until I'n
ready?"

"I promise. Trust me like I trust you."

She was thankful Neil was more trustworthy thar
she'd been initially. The guilt she felt was strong, bu
it couldn't compete with her anticipation as he le
her hands to the snap button of his shorts, and the
the zipper she hesitantly drew down. Tanned ski
gave way to a dark thatch of hair.

"Where's your underwear?"

"Don't wear any. Ever. Not under my street clothe
and not to bed. I like the freedom of movement
nothing binding me. Though I do tend to stay awa
from wool. Take them off?"

His hand massaging her shoulder, he gently presse
her to the floor until he towered over her. His legs, o
either side of her head, were like two great pillars
And then he sprang free and proud, and her mouth
opened in an *O* of astonishment.

Neil possessed an instrument more sleek and
poetic and earthy than any hands could craft. /

thing of beauty that seemed to grow as she, mesmerized, continued to stare.

"So tell me, *chère*, am I to your liking? Or am I your worst nightmare?"

"You are . . ." Andrea swallowed. Then swallowed again. "You're very much to my liking."

"That pleases me. Greatly. You please me, more than greatly. The only thing that would please me more at the moment would be for you to touch me. *There.* Everywhere. While you're on your knees. On your back. On the floor or in bed, I don't care. Just touch me, kiss me, and don't stop, not ever. I need you. You hear me? *I need you.* More than anything. *See* how much I need you. All you're doing is looking and—"

She gripped him, and he was suddenly silent and still. Then he groaned, and it was all the invitation she needed to indulge.

She kissed him. Her kiss was tentative, curious, then grew bold. His buttocks flexed tight as he moved back and forth, guiding her until, shouting her name, he pushed back her forehead with his palm.

"Get up," he said urgently.

"But I don't want to."

"Get up anyway. *Now.*"

"But why? You said I could touch you, taste you. And I want more."

"So do I." His biceps bunched as he hauled her, resistant, to her feet.

The face that greeted hers was tortured, struggling for control. It held no humor, no patience or understanding.

"This is not—" He closed his eyes as if even the sight of her was all it would take to push him over the fine line. "This is not on my résumé."

"You mean a woman hasn't—"

"Of course. A thousand times of course, and then

some. But you're not them, and I'm not me. I haven't been me since the minute I met you."

"Maybe it's the real you underneath the slick veneer."

"There's no veneer here. You're looking at a man who's wishing for once that he hadn't brought some condoms along. I want to say the hell with it, we'll take our chances and worry later. Which is why I'm seeing to this right now."

He quickly reached into his shorts pocket, popped open a blue capsule, and rolled a sheath down his length. As she watched his undisguised actions, she realized she'd let an old man's lust rob her of more than desire. She'd held on to a feeling of shame, a sensation that sex was something dirty. This wasn't dirty. It was natural. Clean. Healthy. A thing of beauty between a man and a woman.

"You're very efficient at doing that," she said, testing this new attitude and quite pleased with the ease she felt.

Neil wiped his brow, appearing relieved for the distraction. "With good reason. I've slept with an assortment of women—nothing to brag about, not when I can't remember most of their names. But one thing I never forget is to protect myself—paternity suits being as much a threat as a social disease."

"You don't think I would threaten you like that, do you?"

"God, no! That's not what I meant atall, *chère*. You're no one-night stand, and no matter where we go from here, I could never forget you." Without warning, his hand slid between her legs. Then his upper lip lifted in a sexy leer. "These cutoffs are fairly well drenched, and I think we'd both feel lots better with them off while we talk about arithmetic."

"Arithmetic?" The glide of his hand, lifting, lifting, until she stood on tiptoe, stole her breath. And then her precarious balance as he worked around bunched denim and panties to swirl a fingertip over her cleft.

"You know, one plus one makes two. Till we get in bed and reverse it—two making one. Of course, there's multiplication. Just curious, but how do you feel about factoring?"

"Ah . . . ah—math wasn't my best subject."

"Seems you could use help. What-say I volunteer to be your tutor? Maybe we'll both learn something before the final exams."

Thirteen

He dropped to his knees. His teeth gripped the bit of denim beside the snap on her shorts and jerked. Andrea stood motionless as the rasp of a zipper being opened filled her ears.

She watched as he rubbed his nose against the deep V of her silk panties, breathing her in deeply until she whimpered and her legs almost gave way while he slowly pulled down the undergarment. Neil tapped her ankles in a silent command for her to step out.

"I see you don't color your hair, *chère*. And it feels as silky as that on your head. Now I have a need to find out if what's behind it is as delicious as the rest of you. Do you mind?"

The fact that he'd asked, when she was quite certain asking wasn't in his résumé any more than talking about his past, touched her. Then he touched her with two broad fingertips, opening her and gently massaging. Into the parted folds he blew a warm stream of air, then kissed her softly.

"May I?" he whispered. "Please."

His slumberous gaze lifted to hers while one large hand came around to stroke her buttocks before tilting her hips forward. Her voice was nowhere to be found, and so she gave a curt nod.

His tongue slid into her.

She'd never been so exposed. Everything that made her a woman was naked, on display for his slitted gaze that held hers, absorbing each raw emotion she felt on her face. She watched him take in each nuance while he took her to a place she'd never been. Taking her there with languorous brushes, then rapid flicks.

Dear Lord, what was happening to her? What was he doing to her? Tears were in her eyes, sliding down her cheeks. It was too much, too overwhelming in its poignance.

And in its pain.

"I hurt, Neil. You're making me hurt."

"Hurt more. With me. I want us to hurt together."

"So good?" she asked, feeling the pain of need. For release. For him. Her body was too empty, and her heart was grasping, contracting in time to her womb that yearned to take him, all of him, until she was full and he was empty.

"It's good," he mouthed against her. "Better than good—it's right." He caught her as her knees buckled, and he shifted his arm beneath them. Lifting her, he quickly strode to the bed and put her down there.

She reached for him, but he remained standing. "Neil?"

"Playtime's over, *chère*. We're getting serious." He went to the coffee table, and in the candlelight she saw a glimmer of silver and gold before he returned, clenching it in his palm.

"What is that?"

"My mouthpiece," he whispered caressing it. "It's made to last, and I take good care of it. That's how I feel about you. And because I do, I'm asking for a special privilege."

"Why?" she asked, gripping the sheet beneath.

"Because this is my soul, something I want touching your body before I put it to my mouth again. I need this from you, and I want to give you something I've never given another. Will you take it? Just the same as taking me, only a lot more personal."

She was beyond words. She was beyond anything but surrendering herself to trust and spreading her arms.

Neil's face was set in somber lines as he straddled her hips and knelt over her. His gaze searched and burned into hers while he pressed a lingering kiss to the mouthpiece.

"Now, you." He grazed it against her lips. "Kiss it," he whispered. "Kiss it and pretend it's me. But you don't have to pretend, not really. Because it is . . . *me*."

Andrea closed her eyes and welcomed the metal with her lips and tongue. His hoarse groan echoed her whimper when he withdrew it from her avid mouth. Wanting to see him, to know if the need she felt pressed against her belly was also in his face, she opened her eyes and saw. . . .

His gaze was trancelike, drawing her deeper into the spell he wove so completely with the wet tip he traced over her chin, down her throat, and then around her breasts. Figure eights he drew, each one smaller than the last until he was circling her nipples. Lingering now, flicking each peak lightly, then not so lightly, and then there was the soft pinch between his thumb and the metal.

A low, keening wail rose from her throat, and there he pressed his tongue. So warm, so wet, so not nearly enough.

As he had pressed her shoulders to urge her to the floor, she pressed his until he kissed his way down and parted her legs with a gentle pressure. Why were they quivering so? she wondered, as something wild and as uncontrolled as the shaking of her legs overtook her.

He bit softly into one inner thigh and then the other, all the while gliding the mouthpiece over her belly, down her legs, then tracing the underside of her crooked knees. He was playing her body, playing it with the same magic he commanded from the instrument he held.

"Feel me," he growled, and parted her for the first sleek stroke. "Do you feel me? Hard and demanding, but for you, only for you. Do you?"

"I feel you," she said brokenly, gripping his head and arching in a demand for more. "Take me. This isn't enough. *Take me.*"

"It would be my pleasure." His mouth was suddenly on her, open and wet and hurting her so good. What he was doing to her would be with her for the rest of her life. How could she ever forget this . . . this unending smooth glide between her legs that called forth a need that was nearly agony, a need he had to fill because she was so empty she was screaming for him to be inside her?

And then he was. She felt the texture of skin, the warmth of flesh, the length of a single finger and then two stroking slowly, carefully. She demanded his fierceness as he continued to glide the mouthpiece over her cleft with a teasing, light brush.

It was a maestro's baton, and *she* was the instrument he played as if she'd been fashioned for his hands only. Sure hands, loving hands that took her higher, higher . . .

So high she soared, her repeated cry of his name proclaiming ecstasy.

Why did it have to end? She grasped to reclaim the wonder, but it was gone . . . except for the tingling glow that lingered like a phantom spirit.

"Andrea," he whispered against her ear. "Open your eyes and look at me."

His smile was intimate and sweet and yet infinitely male. She'd never seen him this way, and somehow she knew the smile was reserved just for her, and her lips answered in kind.

"Thank you, *chère*. Every time I use this, I'll think of you, of now, and play like never before." His gaze, an echo of his smile, held hers as he kissed his mouthpiece. Then he laid it beside her doll before wrapping her in a fierce embrace.

Her head rested against his chest, and she stroked it while he stroked back her hair and tenderly kissed her brow. His palm cupped her hip and urged her leg over his. Andrea's upper thigh, still wet from his kisses, brushed against his groin. He groaned, and she reached to touch him.

Neil caught her wrist and brought it back to his chest.

"Neil?"

"I'm thinking, and I can't think too well when you do that. Why don't you take a little snooze? Don't worry, I'll rouse you before I take off."

Rouse her? Before he left? Just where did he think he was going? And as for taking a little snooze, she had no intentions of nodding off, not when she was aroused.

"Sweet dreams," he murmured silkily. "Oh, and about that possibility we were discussin' earlier? It has become a most certain certainty. I *do* love you. Nighty-night, *chère*."

"Neil," she groaned, "I can't go to sleep. I don't even *want* to go to sleep."

"Then what do you want?"

"What do you *think* I want?" she panted, ready to throw him on his back, mount him, and *take* what he was withholding. "Make love to me, Neil. Sweet heaven, what are you waiting for?"

His dark laughter filled her ear as his shadowed face loomed over hers. "Somewhere between body shots and now I realized just how much I need you in my world. Maybe more than you could ever need me in yours. What am I waiting for? A sign from you that we've got a most mutual need."

"A *sign*? What are you looking for? A billboard, skywriting? Of course it's mutual. I *need* you. All of you. In my life. And in my body. *Now*."

"You're sure?"

"Yes, I'm sure! What do you want me to do, beg?"

"Music to my ears. Beg for me?" He kissed her hard and madly until she tore her mouth from his. "*Beg for me*. Say please. Please, Neil, I love you and I want you. Tonight. Tomorrow. I need you so much that I'll die if you leave."

"Don't leave," she pleaded. "Never leave. Please. I love you. I want you, all of you—"

"Are you really sure? It's important that you know the rest of the equation before answering."

Somehow she realized this was a power play, a glimpse into a future that involved a man who liked to call the shots in and out of bed.

"What's your game?" she demanded haltingly.

"No game. I want to strike a deal. I'll cut down my drinking, maybe even the smokes. As for other women, they don't exist. In exchange you put up with my moods, which, as you know, can be taxing. *And* you share my bed. I do tend to be quite taxing there too. If you can live with that, I do believe we can live together. Say . . . my place? Just till I get this one fixed up. I'll be glad to help you pack in the mornin'. If you need some time to think, I can leave."

He rolled off her, and she grabbed him back. Her legs twined around his. He lay flush on top and teased her with a small nudge that placed him barely inside.

"How—how can you be so manipulative?" She bit his shoulder in outrage, in passion.

"Ohhh, that's good. A bit more than a nip, but not

hard enough to draw blood. Just the way I like it. I believe you deserve a little reward, learning so fast." He rocked forward slightly, and she cried for more of him.

"Sorry," he murmured, "as much as I'd love to oblige, I'm still in need of your answer."

"Damn you, Neil! *Damn you.* You set me up! I don't believe it. How could . . . after . . . you conniving, unscrupulous bastard, you actually set me up!"

"My, what a colorful vocabulary you have. Not that I blame you for giving me a tongue-lashing—and such a talented tongue it is—since I am guilty as charged. But, Andrea, surely you realize this wasn't easy for me, coming here tonight. We're talking a very big compromise. I'm asking you to meet me halfway."

"And if I refuse?"

"Then we've got a real problem on our hands. And till it's worked out, best we sleep in separate beds."

"You'd actually be cruel enough to leave me like this?"

"Aw no, *chère.* I'm afraid I'd do something crueler. *This.*" He claimed her fully with a sudden quick jerk.

Her cry was sharp and fierce. It came from her soul and emerged from her lips. "*Neil . . . Neil . . .* "

"Here, *chère.* Here I am and here I belong. Here, where you belong to me. But only for tonight. Unless you accept that I want the best for you because *I love you.*" His lips hovered over hers, then his tongue lapped tears from her cheeks. "Be a good sport and don't fight me on this. I know I'm selfish, but you're being selfish too. Let me think of someone besides myself for a change."

She crushed her lips against his with a sob of defeat. "All right. All right! We'll do it your way. Are you satisfied?"

"With your answer, yes. Otherwise . . . *no.*" He groaned low as he began to move inside her. "Hold my hand. Tight as you're holding me inside." A broad palm spread over hers, and she locked her fingers with his. "I'll lead the first steps until you know them by heart. Dance with me?"

As Billie Holiday crooned another song, Neil guided her with such fluid grace that she found herself moving effortlessly to an increasingly rapid beat. His praise burned hot and sweet in her ears, in her breast, compelling her on until she was soaring again, higher than before.

His heart beat above hers, no longer in a gentle persuasion but in a rough rise and fall as they galloped together in the joy of unrestrained passion. The more she gave, the more he gave back. She took him. And took him. And took him until she thought he might tear her into fragments of ecstasy.

And then he did. She cried at the beauty of it. She covered his face with kisses, which he returned until he wrenched his mouth away and lunged forward.

He stared down at her as she felt the pulse of his release. He came in a stunning silence. He came in absolute stillness, not even with a blink.

Andrea began to shiver, unsure if it was from the chilled air that fanned over their sweat-slick bodies or his continued stare, as if he were in shock.

"Neil?" She touched his cheek, and he softly bit her palm. "Are you okay?"

"I don't think so."

"What's wrong? Please, tell me."

"Math," he whispered.

"I don't understand, Neil."

"It's very simple, *chère*. Simple as two halves making a whole."

Neil studied his surroundings as he blew another smoke ring into the early morning light.

A roach skittered across the floor in the kitchenette.

The avocado-green refrigerator in the corner wheezed for another breath while Billie Holiday sounded as if she needed a rest from the automatic replay.

It wasn't only Billie's voice that needed a rest. Neil pulled Andrea closer and was amazed to feel that part of him that should have needed a rest stir. He stroked Andrea's hair away from her face and studied her profile.

He'd never been more sober. Sober and eager to have Andrea in tow when he crawled out of bed. The mattress beneath them was thin, and at least ten springs had unhinged since they'd taken each other on. But the sheets were clean—if he didn't count the sweat now on it or the faint streak of blood that he'd discovered earlier. He'd blinked and blinked again, while he groped with the realization that he'd been Andrea's first, not the second.

It had certainly been a first for him, making love to a woman he loved. A woman he had the good sense God gave him to never let go.

"Seems I stand corrected," he whispered. "You and Lou were both right, *chère*. It don't matter where a person rests his head, so long as he wakes up next to the right person."

While the refrigerator hummed and Billie Holiday sang on, Neil lifted a candle stub from beside the bed and took a shot at the roach.

He laughed quietly. "Bull's-eye."

His next target might not be as easy: Getting a ring on Andrea's finger and the first of their children in her belly before summer was out.

He'd give them everything he'd been deprived of, the things he still craved, his very own *Father Knows Best* home. Yet he couldn't lie to himself. Even in this he was being a selfish bastard. He wanted to be the breadwinner, the sole provider, for all the right reasons, but there was one that wasn't exactly noble.

Fear. Fear of losing her, whether it was to another man, to death, or even a career. All the things that had shaped his life and him into what he was: a man who loved her, needed her so desperately that he would use any means to keep her tied to him.

Fourteen

"You're fired."

"I'm *what*?"

Without bothering to look up from his ledger, Neil said matter-of-factly, "You're fired. F-I-R-E-D. As in, fired."

"Did I just hear you say that I'm fired?"

"As of tonight, you are no longer tending bar."

"As of tonight, I'm *no longer* tending bar!"

"Is there an echo in here or *what*?" Pushing back his chair from the desk, he stretched, then popped the suspenders riding his shoulders. He looked at her then, a sly smile on his lips. "Another bartender starts tonight, the one who's taking your place. You've got a new job, *chère*. The club manager quit, and guess who's taking his position?"

Andrea eyed Neil warily. If she'd learned anything in the past few weeks of sharing a pillow with him, it was that he was a master chess player—another of his attributes he hadn't mentioned but made sure she found out about. Whether at the game board or the bedroom or in this immaculate office she couldn't believe was the same one they'd first met in, he called every checkmate. It was his game, and anyone who challenged it left with nothing, not even a shirt.

"I don't know anything about running a club, Neil."

"Not yet. But if you pick up how to run a club as fast as you did bartending, then you'll be the best club manager this side of the Mason-Dixon Line. Besides, I can't concentrate while every man at the bar's hitting on you."

So that was it. He'd already thrown out several patrons, cutting short a few numbers to do it.

"This is ridiculous. How many times do I have to tell you that I can take care of myself? I've more than learned the best way to deal with a drunk." A state she'd yet to see him in. Not only had he cut his smoking in half, his drinking was down to a trickle.

Still, that didn't make him an easy man to live with, although he did accept her explanation of the typewriter she'd taken to his house—that it had been a graduation present. More than that, he was always sober, surprisingly neat—and not a day went by that he didn't bring her fresh flowers or a trinket she'd admired. For some reason his nonstop gift-giving bothered her, so she'd quit pointing out whatever caught her eye—not that it stopped him from showering her with presents anyway.

"Don't matter if you can deal with a drunk. Proprietor's prerogative. We'll work on the books together tomorrow. Tonight, we'll work on each other." He glanced at his watch. "I've got an hour before I need to warm up. Practice making perfect, how about an early start? I'm already hot."

He reached for his sax and slipped loose the mouthpiece. Andrea edged toward the closed door of his office.

"That's far enough, Neil. Put it down."

"Make me. Or better yet, I'll make you." As he stroked it between thumb and middle finger, her knees wobbled, and she steadied herself against the wall.

He tossed the mouthpiece to his desk and, with a quick stride, reached her and slid his hand up her skirt. She'd begun to wear skirts lately at his request. One of many requests she'd agreed to. Like the one that had her sharing his bed while her apartment floor swarmed with carpenters and plumbers and electricians. They were toppling walls, reclaiming hardwood floors, replacing light fixtures. And the bathroom! Black marble tile wrapped around a sleek sunken tub, and a bidet.

"Gets you every time, *chère*. Good thing I don't have the same problem onstage, or it could be a very embarrassing situation." He smiled as her nails sank into his wrist, and he tightened his intimate grip. "Why, Andrea, what a good sport you are. Usually, it takes at least five minutes before you start to claw. Ten to bite. You're making excellent progress, and I most certainly approve."

"Sink your teeth into this, Slick. I have no desire to be your club manager. You'll have to hire someone else."

"Then where will you work?"

"Behind the bar, of course."

"No such thing. I don't want you tending anymore, not here, not anywhere. Do I make myself clear?"

"Yes, you do. Now I'm making myself clear. I've worked hard to learn the ropes. I'm fast, the clientele likes me—"

"Too much, that's the problem."

"I'm a good bartender, Neil."

"The best."

"Then you have no right to take away my position."

"I claim the right, as the man who loves you and sleeps with you, to enjoy any position the two of us can devise. The wall's right handy, but the couch is a mite more comfortable. Take your pick, unless you want me to choose. Say, both?"

"Forget either unless you've got something better to offer than trying to bully me into a job that I don't want."

"Lord, but you do drive a hard bargain." He sighed and shook his head. "I was afraid of this, so I did give some thought to another arrangement. Come park them sweet little buns on my lap, *chère*."

When she refused to budge, he picked her up and moved to the couch, where he nuzzled her neck and murmured sweet, naughty nothings into her ear until she slumped against him with a sigh. Here they go again, she thought, bracing herself. He wanted something and knew exactly what strings to pull to get it, which included shifting her thighs until she was straddling his hips.

"Go ahead, Neil. Lay it on me while I'm still coherent."

"Okay, try this on for size. You don't tend bar, and you don't manage the club. Instead, you manage yours truly."

Could it be? She'd seen the amazing volume of work he put out, often writing in a frenzy as she looked on from the bed.

"You mean you're ready to record again? To tour?"

"Have you been drinking what I haven't? Since you moved in, my muse seems to think I've got a machine gun for a brain. I need a rest, not an ulcer. I'm talking about something much more appealing than me coming out of the closet and firing one of those sure hits you've inspired me to crank out."

Something more appealing than what she'd subtly been pushing for? "This I have to hear."

"Here's the deal. You quit working and spend your free time decorating. Thanks to all the bucks I'm shelling out for overtime labor, the third floor'll be done before summer's out. It's gonna have lots of style, but it'll need a woman's touch. Your touch. A touch I need worse than our home does. I want you sitting at the front table every night while I play each song for you. And while some other club manager closes up the bar, we'll tear up the sheets, then watch a rerun of *Father Knows Best*." His gaze searched hers as he said softly, "I would like to be a father. The kind of father I always dreamed of having. With you as the mother, better than the best."

Andrea groped for words, while his words echoed between her ears.

"I—um, I'd prefer to be married first, Neil."

"That could be arranged."

"But—but we haven't known each other long enough."

"Long enough for me to know that I love you like crazy, and I'll do whatever it takes to keep you. Do you know what it means to me to be the one who makes you smile and wakes you up with a kiss every mornin'? What a deep sense of pride I feel, being able to take care of you? Let me. Let me make you as happy as you make me."

He *couldn't* be proposing this soon. Despite Liza's warning, she wasn't prepared. Neil wanted a wife who made *him* her career, while he kept his own and thrived on her total dependence on him. The kind of dependence that had made his mother weak. It was a weakness that he saw as strength.

Andrea knew he loved her. Passionately. So passionately, his love was all-consuming. He held on too tight, as if certain she'd desert him if he let her loose. Knowing what she did of his past, she understood. But she had to make *him* understand that love couldn't be caged or bought with lavish gifts. What she wanted, *needed*, was his trust. Trust so absolute she had no fear of *his* desertion once she confessed her deception.

She needed even more: his support of her chosen career. She was, would always be, a journalist. Oh, how he loathed the press, and she probably would, too, had her life been held up to public ridicule and titillation. But she wasn't Neil, and she couldn't give up her profession any more than she could give up her love for him. Did he love her enough to accept that? Could their whirlwind affair compete with his lifetime of distrust?

Sadly, she doubted it. *Time.* They needed time.

"I'm sorry, Neil," she said slowly. "I love you, more each day, but I can't live in a gilded cage. That's not real, and it's not enough. Not for me."

"Then what do you want? I couldn't deny you a thing, *chère.* Everything I have, all that I am—such as that is—is yours. Problem is, there's a part of me that wants to put you in that gilded cage along with the children we're going to have."

Andrea took a deep breath. "Did you miss me this afternoon?"

"I did. Where was—were you?"

"At the doctor."

"You're not sick are you? Tell me you're not sick."

"No. I went for the reason we're discussing."

His fervent expression of concern eased into an expectant smile. "*Chère*, you're not—"

"No, Neil. I'm not pregnant. My period was late, so I went to have it checked out. The results were negative, and I left with a prescription for birth-control pills."

His smile went flat, and the spark in his eyes died.

"I see," he said dully.

"Quite the contrary, I don't think that you see at all."

"Then why don't you get busy and enlighten me?" he snapped. How quickly he could turn, and it only increased her apprehension.

"All right, I will. I grew up in an orphanage, always wanting a home and two parents who loved me. Things most children take for granted."

"Not me."

"I realize that. And so you, of *all* people, should understand what it means to conceive a child, to give him or her the advantage of stability, a home where the parents might disagree but aren't at terrible odds."

"We don't fight!"

"Not lately, but as of now we're making up for lost time." She shoved a finger into his chest and her face into his. "Get this, Neil, and get it good. I've taken your laundry to the cleaners and cooked your meals—"

"I've cooked just as many for you. I thought you liked my grits at breakfast. The only thing you said you liked better was my jambalaya. And even if I don't get the clothes washed I have bought you several dresses to make up for the ones I've ripped in my hurry to get you naked."

"That's beside the point. I want more in my life than to tend a man who has a career, or what remains of it."

"What the hell does that have to do with you and me and our future?"

"A lot, Neil. It has to do with you not liking what you ended up with after climbing the path to the top. Once you were there, the room with a view didn't look out on what you'd envisioned. So what did you do?"

"Changed it, that's what."

"Yes, that's exactly what you did. Made horrible scenes in public, didn't show for concerts—"

"I told you, my life had already gone sour, but when the music stopped, I lost my want to please a crowd. So what if a few fans had to get tickets refunded?"

"A few people? Try Carnegie Hall, sold out, while you checked into a ratty motel with a bottle and a gun. Thank God you called Lou to tell him good-bye—long enough for him to trace the call and fly in just in time to drag you back home. If recent memory serves, you did say that you were sick for a week and haven't left New Orleans since."

"Saw enough of the world to last me a lifetime,

hanks. No reason for me to leave when my lawyers
could take care of the bloody mess." He grinned,
making light of the horror that time had apparently
diluted for him but not for her, never for her. "Picked
that bloody word up on tour in England."

She sighed. "The point is, *they* took care of *your*
mess. You didn't want to deal with it, so you paid
someone else to so you could stick your head in the
sand. How irresponsible."

"It most certainly wasn't! I survived the only way I
knew how. And as for paying somebody else to deal
with my legal messes, wise up. That's how it's done
in the real world. Believe me, all involved were well
compensated."

"That's another thing that bothers me. *Money.* You
and your damn money. You've got more than you
know what to do with, and you won't even hire a
personal accountant. And why?"

"Because it's mine, and as such it's my right to
count it, invest it, and spend it how I see fit. You grew
up poor, so surely you can understand my fondness
for keeping my own books. What's your beef with
that? I'm generous with you."

"*Too* generous. Did it possibly occur to you that
sometimes I might want to use *my* money? Or that
your open-coffer policy robs me of the right to contribute?"

"Ain't no need for you to do that. I've got plenty for
us both."

"That's *not* the issue. Look, your money is a security blanket for you, and I empathize with that. But
you have to understand that I want some security of
my own."

"What I understand is that I'll make sure you
never lack for money *or* security. But since you want
to fend for yourself, I'll give you a tip. Money is a very
powerful tool. So's the truth. They got me a divorce
and out of a record contract the label's CEO had
plenty of incentive to wash his hands of. Seems he

didn't want his dirt aired by those rags that lap that stuff right up."

Andrea shifted uneasily, feeling an incriminating blush stain her cheeks. The more he confided, the more her charade became worthy of punishment. She knew too much, and she knew him too well. Neil's core was hard, and he never forgave a betrayal. She shivered as her heart raced.

"What are you getting at?"

"The moral is, you don't seem to trust me enough yet to let me protect you and provide for your future. I, on the other hand, trust you. I've given you the means to provide for yourself at my expense. You could always write a story about me that would tide you over for some time."

Andrea felt like the fraud she was, pointing the finger at Neil's character weaknesses while desperately covering her own. She was a liar, a cheat. Worse, she was a coward, terrified of losing his love.

"So tell me, *chère*," he said, stripping off her shirt and bra, "what does all this have to do with you getting on the Pill because you don't want my babies any more than you want to settle down with me?"

"It's not that I don't want to."

"Then what is it?"

Fear, Neil, she wanted to scream. *Knee-knocking, dry-heaves fear. I'm afraid to relinquish what independence I still have left, afraid of what you'll do once I tell you the truth. I can't marry you with this lie between us, the lie and the damning evidence of it that grows with each page I type.*

God, how she wanted to tell him that. She *had* to before they could take the next step. The fact that she couldn't was proof their relationship needed time to mature. But at least she could offer him a portion of truth.

"You tried to control me, Neil. Me and our future, with the same kind of tunnel vision that took you to the top. It's a variation on the theme. You want

something, and you do whatever it takes to get it.
And once you've got it, what happens if the reality
doesn't live up to the dream? I don't think I could
survive if you discarded me like Christine. "

"I'd *never* do that," he vowed solemnly.

"I pray it's true, Neil. But I need time to be sure
that what we have is strong enough to overcome any
test."

"And just how long might *that* be?"

"I don't know," she said, distress sounding in her
voice. "Long enough for me to work out a few things
for myself. Long enough for you to adjust to the fact
that I'm not cut out to be Donna Reed. I'd rather be
Old Mother Hubbard—"

"Especially if I give you my bone?"

She laughed to keep from crying. Neil could always
make her laugh, even now, when she wanted to weep
because everything was so wrong. "You have the
raunchiest sense of humor of any person I've ever
met."

"One of my finer qualities, judging from the way
those pretty pink nipples of yours are puckered up
and begging for a kiss. And you did tell me my sense
of humor was one reason I'm the sexiest, most
irresistible man you've ever made love to."

"You're the *only* man I've ever made love to."

"I'm the only man you ever *will* make love with." He
speared her with a possessive gaze as he rolled her to
her back. His lips were tight, and his eyes were
narrowed in a dangerous squint. "The *only* man,
chère. Never betray me, never lie to me . . . and
never forget it."

Fifteen

"It's summer's end, and you still ain't got a ring on yo' finger," Liza said, snorting with disgust. "Honey, I just don't believe it. My predictions always come true. Guess that man's not as smart as I gave him credit for." She sighed wistfully as she spread her arms to encompass the bedroom. "Then again, he do deserve some credit for turning a sow into a swan if this floor looked anything like the other two in the works."

"It is beautiful, isn't it, Liza?" Andrea took inventory of her new surroundings. From the stucco walls and arched picture windows to the Bukhara carpet and the exquisite furniture that hugged it, she stared in awe.

Until her gaze came to rest on the carved chest of drawers that housed those typewritten pages. She ached to share them with Neil, whose acceptance was essential before they could say "I do."

"This here's more than beautiful," Liza asserted. "It's a declaration of his love for you that says a ring comes next."

"We'll see. He has been known to change his mind—I'm still tending bar. And I—I'm afraid there's a chance he might decide otherwise about wanting to marry me too."

"Is that why you be wearing that 'woe is me' look on yo' face? Lawd, can't you see he's crazy about you? He ain't gonna get cold feet at this late date. Neil's finally got his head on straight and his act together. Thanks be to you."

"But, Liza, he could change. I'm so scared he's going to change."

"Just what heck are you talking about?" Liza's brow furrowed into lines of concern as tears filled Andrea's eyes. She grasped Andrea's trembling fingers and said kindly, "What's the trouble, chile? You can tell Liza. I promise it won't go no further, not even to Lou."

Andrea needed no more encouragement to sob against the older woman's shoulder. She felt a loving hand pat her back in a motherly consolation she needed now more than ever.

"Liza, I don't know what to do. I don't know what Neil will do when he finds out. I didn't mean to betray him, but he has to know. And—and once he does, he . . . Oh God, Christine was unfaithful. I've been unfaithful too. Worse than she was, Liza. Because he loves me, and he never really loved her. I'm afraid he won't forgive me. Maybe I have broken his rules, but he can break my heart. He never forgets a right or a wrong done to him, and he can be so cruel, so blind. I'm terrified, Liza. I thought time would help, but—but the only thing it's done is opened him up, and the more he tells me, the guiltier I look. What am I going to do, Liza? That's why I turned him down when he proposed, kind of, and—"

"Calm down, chile. You ain't making a lick of sense. C'mon now, let's sit and have us a heart-to-heart."

Almost an hour later, as they sat on the bed amid a heap of soaked tissues, Liza's sympathetic groans became a weary shake of the head.

"Lawd, honey, but you do have a mess of squiggling worms in a beat-up can. Where's that thing you wrote?"

"In my drawer. Under the pills Neil told me to keep out of his sight."

"Seems to me, you don't have much choice, if marriage is what you want. You did say that Neil had chilled out on his uncool ideas? That you have a right to your own career?"

"Well . . . yes. Not that he likes it, but he respects me enough to accept it and support what I want to do. Only he doesn't have an inkling of what that really is. I'm a journalist, Liza. It's in my blood and always will be. Like Neil. How am I ever going to reconcile one with the other?"

Liza patted Andrea's hand. "Ain't no two ways about it. You're gonna have to gut up, gal."

"You mean tell him the truth? Tell him I wormed my way into his confidence to get a story, then changed my mind? I'm scared to death he won't listen, that he'll accuse me of setting him up, then shut me out. We've known each other less than four months. How can that possibly compete with his past? It's twisted him."

"He's been twisted fo' sho', but you've done strung him up and turned him inside out. He's set on making you his wife. This here place proves that what you two've got is strong and good. Leastwise, it's a sure sign that's what Neil believes. How come you don't look around you and believe it too?"

"Because 'this here place' is part of the problem. Neil knows how to show his love through money, and I've got jewelry, paintings, clothes, and dolls to prove it. His trust isn't so freely given. *Trust.* It's something he thinks we have, but we don't. I don't trust him enough to spill my guts, and once I do, the trust he has in me could be shattered."

"Hmmm . . . guess you've got a point. Let me think a spell. You sure he won't find it? You'd look ten times worse if he came upon it, like you was hiding something instead of taking it on yo'self to show him."

"He won't find it. We shook on never going through each other's things without permission. And as you know, once Neil gives his word, it's etched in stone. He believes in privacy and trust as much as he hates cheats."

"That he does. They're right up there with liars and unfaithful wives. The problem you say you've got is that you qualify for one and hit the gray line with the other. But now that I've given this some thought—"

"You have an idea?" Andrea urgently asked.

"Not exactly. Just a good dose of common sense. Seems to me you been hidin' them secrets so long you can't stand 'em no more. But you don't know when to tell him. Listen to yo' heart, honey. It always tells the truth. You'll know when the time's right, for you and him both."

Andrea kissed Liza's cheek. "Thank you, Liza. Thank you for listening and understanding."

"Oh, fiddle-dee-dee, gal. I thank you for loving our son and giving him the home you both deserve. Come to think of it, it's a good thing you like to write. That could be a point in your favor, having a career where you could mostly stay at home. Even Slick couldn't argue with that."

"I hope so, Liza. I do hope so."

Neil bounded up the steps to the bedroom, whistling his latest tune. One of his best, even if he did say so himself. In the two months since he and Andrea had moved into their third-floor love nest, he'd written enough for a year. It kept coming and coming, as if he'd tapped into a rich, bottomless well.

And all of it was pure gold. The kind of stuff he could sell for a mint—but didn't. Why, he wasn't exactly sure, but somehow it was too personal to let anyone else have it for any price. He couldn't let it go.

Wishing Andrea would hurry up and come home, he hung up his fall coat next to the cashmere cape he'd bought her recently. Late October was a colorful time of year in New Orleans, though it couldn't compare with the tint of Andrea's cheeks that of late had deepened to a rosy glow.

Reaching into his shirt pocket, he withdrew two plane tickets. First class, like his woman. He checked the departure date. Two weeks from today. They'd be in New England in time to see the magnificent fall foliage. Not that he planned to let her out for long from the honeymoon suite he'd reserved—under the name of Mr. and Mrs. Neil Grey.

He wasn't about to take no for an answer. Besides, he had no reason to expect anything but a yes. Since that night he'd fired her and rehired her, he hadn't asked again. Andrea, however, had been dropping hints like crazy.

"Neil, I've been thinking that I'd rather work at something besides tending bar. I like to write, and I'm pretty good at it, and if I could make a go of it, it's the kind of job that would let me spend more time at home . . ."

He smiled, the same big grin he'd worn when the jeweler had handed over the custom-designed ring. Neil fished the box from his pocket. Right pretty, he thought, the way it was wrapped in shimmery foil and topped with a cascade of ribbon. Red, just as he'd asked, to match her hair.

Neil went to the chest of drawers and looked at himself in the mirror. He could use a shave, but Andrea said she liked his night shadow; his whisker burn excited her. He'd let his hair grow out again, but the barber had shaped it nicely.

"Just look at you," he said to his reflection. "If you ain't a cool cat on a hot streak, getting all fixed up for woman who's got you shuttin' the toilet lid and picking up her underwear to boot."

He laughed softly. Andrea wasn't a slob by any means, but he did seem to pick up after her more than she did him. They'd probably need to hire a housekeeper once they started having babies.

Every time he passed the sleek mahogany banister, he imagined standing at the foot of it while a little voice shouted, "Daddy! Daddy!" then slid down to his waiting arms. Then Andrea would greet him with a kiss while they all hugged.

There'd be fights for sure, and days when nothing went right. He knew that. Hell, he'd been a realist a lot longer than a man who was claiming his dream. But if he could have his dream, he could handle whatever got thrown his way. If he'd had that sooner, he'd likely still be recording.

The thought tugged at him, but he shook it off. Right now he had a proposal to rehearse.

Clearing his throat, Neil began, "Andrea, I have been patient, but my patience has run out. We're getting married, and I've got a ring here that says so. I did spend a small fortune on it, and they do have a no-return policy. . . ."

That didn't come out right. Best he try again.

"Andrea, *chère*. I love you more than words can say. You're the music in my life, the song in my heart. Do me the honor of wearing this ring, and be more than my friend and lover. Say you'll be my wife."

Nah, too sappy. Maybe he should forget the words and make it a surprise. He did that a lot, leaving a rose on her pillow, whisking her downstairs to a waiting horse and carriage, or tucking a little something into a clothes pocket so that next time she wore it she'd discover the keepsake inside.

He needed a special hiding place, one that she was sure to go to tonight. Tomorrow wouldn't do; his

insides were hopping like Mexican jumping beans a
it was.

Clothes—no telling what she'd wear when. Unde
her pillow—no good either, since he had plans t
make it official before they celebrated in bed. Mayb
the refrigerator where he had champagne chilling
Didn't seem too romantic putting a ring next t
leftover red beans and rice.

Then where? She'd see it right away on the burea
top where the tickets rested.

Neil's gaze dropped a few inches to her lingeri
drawer. He didn't poke around in there, not even t
put in laundry or any of the nighties he'd bought or
impulse upon imagining how she'd look in some sex
next-to-nothing garment. They'd shaken on trustin,
each other never to go through the other's things.

Hmmm. So what if he bent the rules a tad? Once sh
saw what he'd placed in there—the ultimate symbo
of his trust and love and respect—well . . . surel
she wouldn't mind. He'd gladly return the favor
After all, husbands and wives shared everything
There was no room for secrets. He'd certainly share
most of his.

Hell, maybe after tonight they'd even share draw
ers. His suspenders tangled up with her panties'
Yowzah, he did like that idea—and the naughty idea:
it stirred.

Neil winked at his image, then slid out Andrea'
top drawer and promptly decided that she *was* a
slob.

"What a mess." He chuckled, sifting his fingers
through lacy bras, garter belts, and French stock
ings, all mixed up with teddies, slips, and chemises
most of which he'd bought. If he straightened out the
sexy contents, she'd probably even thank him. Be
sides, from the looks of the drawer, she could go a
week and miss the ring.

Neil gathered a handful of feminine garments and
inhaled the scent of lemon and lavender as he

pressed his nose into satin and silk. He tossed it to the bed and filled his hands with a second batch. With the third scoop he emptied the drawer . . . and saw a stack of typewritten pages.

His brow furrowed, Neil pitched aside the lingerie. He wasn't a cheat, and his relationship with Andrea was based on trust, so as curious as he was, he denied the urge to read what was on the pages— except he'd already seen the cover page.

Three lines in clear black letters he couldn't believe:

Neil Grey, Man or Myth?
by
Andrea Post

Sixteen

Fingers numb, Neil picked up the pages.

He felt cold, so cold that ice water seemed to rush in his veins, circulate through shivering muscles and pool in his chest.

Neil replaced the unread pages exactly where he'd found them. Didn't matter what they said. Didn't even matter that he'd been a stupid dupe who spilled his secrets on the pillow he shared with her eager ears. Didn't matter if she'd planted a tape recorder to save herself the trouble of taking notes.

Didn't matter because she'd said she loved him. But that must have been a lie, too, because if she *truly* loved him, the way he loved her, she never would have played him for a sucker. Such a sucker he'd renounced the Vow, gotten into her head and lost his, listened to her cheating heart and served his to her on a platter of trust.

He'd played it straight with Andrea, laid the rules out nice and clean: Love without trust didn't exist for him. Didn't take a mathematician to figure out where that left them.

He turned to the bed, mechanically picking up her things that had lost all sense of familiarity. Strange. But maybe not. They did belong to an intimate stranger. The Andrea he knew wasn't capable of deceit, of betrayal. Of saying she loved him to his face while she stabbed him in the back with her pen.

He watched his motions as if from a distance, as if his hands were detached from the rest of him. Neil felt a sudden urge to wash them and hurried to finish, then went to the bathroom and soaped up. He began to shiver. Had to borrow some warmth to stop his crazy shaking.

Neil reached into his back pocket. Where the hell was that flask? Oh yeah, he didn't carry it with him anymore.

He headed to the entertainment room and latched on to a bottle of brandy at the bar. The damn thing wouldn't cooperate with him long enough for him to pour. Who needed a glass anyway?

His gaze wandered across the room to an original painting he and Andrea had fallen in love with and had hung on the wall with care. His hand shot out to hurl the glass, and the sound of crystal shattering against canvas, then falling like jagged tears, broke his trance.

With a harsh, ugly laugh he grabbed the bottle and returned to the bedroom, drinking as he went.

Sinking into a chair, he fixed his unseeing gaze on the open bedroom door.

The shaking stopped. The coldness became a seething heat.

Neil put aside the bottle. And he waited.

Andrea unlocked the front door. A coward no more, she knew it was now or never. She'd "gut up" as Liza had wisely urged, and then pray that everything would work out. Even if her history with Neil wasn't nearly as long as his past, surely they'd had long enough for him to hear her out.

She had no choice but to bet on the strength of their

love and his trust. He had to listen—and believe—her side of the story.

And once he did, she would tell him. Tell him the most wonderful news that she still couldn't believe herself.

"Neil! Neil! Where are you?" Andrea walked up the stairs, her heart doing a tap dance. At the open door to the bedroom, she stopped. The curtains were closed against the waning light outside.

She saw him lounging in the chair as he struck a match against the sole of his shoe, then touched the flames to the cigarette drooping negligently between his lips.

His sleeves were rolled up, and his shirt was undone. He looked relaxed and yet coiled tight. He looked sexy and lethal.

"Neil?"

"That's my name."

"What are you doing?"

"Waiting. For you." His voice was too soft and flat.

She watched as he tapped his ashes, and they fell onto the new rug next to the open bottle standing within reach of his fingers. His casual action contradicted the steely glint in his narrowed eyes.

"Are you drunk?"

"No."

"Something's wrong."

"It is? Care to tell me what that could be?"

"I—I don't know. You tell me."

He put the cigarette in his mouth and tossed off his shirt.

"Tell you what, *chère*, I'm in the mood for a little game. You're so good at humoring me when I think these things up for us two. You know, *private* things that no one else is meant to share. Nothing wrong with that when a man and woman love and trust each other, right?"

The hair on her nape grew damp, and her lips trembled as they formed an answer. "Right," she said uncertainly.

"Make you a deal. Play my game, and then I'll tell you what's up after it's over. Fair enough?"

Had he found out about the article? He couldn't have unless— Her gaze darted from him to the chest of drawers. Surely, he wouldn't have gone through her personal things, not the way he coveted his own privacy.

"I'm waiting," he said quietly. "Can't play by myself. C'mon, *chère*, be a good sport. I have a surprise for you, but you have to be game to get it. Are you in?"

His voice was smooth as glass, the smile he flashed her chilling. Or was guilt causing her to imagine it?

"Okay, I'm in," she hesitantly agreed. "I suppose you have rules."

"Of course. You know how I like to play everything straight. And, like you, I never cheat." He picked up the bottle and took a long swig, then lit another cigarette from the butt of the previous one and rose. Standing at the chest of drawers, he caught her gaze in the mirror, then his eyes glanced down to rest on the polished wood top. Andrea followed their path and saw the tiny wrapped box.

Of course! Why hadn't she guessed? Leave it to Neil to turn an ordinary proposal into a game complete with rules.

"This is how we play. I give you a command, but before you follow it, you say, 'Neil, may I?' If I say, 'You may' then you may. If I say 'You may not,' then you may not. Like 'Mother May I?' Sweet and simple as my command that you take four steps forward."

Andrea stepped forward, meaning to throw her arms around him and call his hand. Her own hands were eager to open what had to be a jeweler's box with a ring meant for her finger. But first she had to confess.

"Neil, I—"

"Wrong!" He laughed. "It's 'Neil, *may* I?' Return to

your place and stay there till you understand the rules." He blew a smoke ring and winked in the mirror. "Let's try it again, *chère*. Take four steps forward."

"Neil . . . may I?"

"You may. Very good. Now, you *may* say, 'Neil, I love you and I trust you, just as you have loved and trusted me, and more than anything I want to kiss you and never stop.'"

"I love you and I trust you, just as you do me, and more than anything I do want to kiss you and never stop."

"Then what are you waiting for? I would so like a kiss."

As he turned to face her, she rushed to him and wrapped her arms around his bare waist. Why did he feel different to her touch? And why were his lips hard and remote as he possessed her mouth and his hands moved over her body? He undressed her quickly but not with the same white-hot heat that usually consumed their patience with loving preliminaries. There was a cold efficiency in his disrobing of her now, and she felt no emotion in the fingertips that roved over her nakedness.

"You *may* lie down on the bed," he softly commanded. "Facedown and palm up." When she hesitated, he reached for the box. He tossed it in the air, then caught it as he stared at her with a teasing, taunting smile.

"Neil, I—I don't think I like this game anymore. We need to talk."

"Later. You know what's in here, don't you? I do so want you to open it. C'mon, *chère*. Let me have my fun."

Never taking her eyes off Neil, she cautiously moved to the bed and lay down as he'd instructed.

He held the box just out of her reach while he traced her spine with his fingers, then patted her behind. Several times, very tenderly. Andrea flinched as if he'd struck her.

Finally, he placed the box on her palm. "Unwrap what I bought just for you."

With shaking hands she started to untie the ribbon.

"Uh-uh-uh. You forgot . . . Neil, may I?"

Dear God how she wanted this horrid game to end. She realized then what it was. A calculated game of cat-and-mouse designed to trap her for her wrongdoing. *He knew.*

"You found it, didn't you?" she said, forcing the words from her lips.

"Found what, *chère?* Have you got a surprise for me too? No, don't tell me, or you might spoil mine. Hurry up now, you *may* open my surprise so you can give me yours. Let's get this over with, so we can quit playing and get to business."

She couldn't get it over with soon enough. Tearing off the ribbon, she glanced up at Neil. His grim, hard gaze raked over her prone body as he drank freely from the bottle, then swiped his forearm over his lips.

"Open it."

"Neil, may—"

"Dammit, yes."

Her hands like ice, she unwrapped the jeweler's box and lifted the top. And then she was gazing at a stunning heart-shaped five-carat diamond set in gold. The gemstone had a pink cast, which contrasted with the crystal-clear teardrop-shaped diamonds that radiated from it like sunbeams. It was breathtaking. One of a kind.

"You may now say, 'It's beautiful, Neil, and I wish I could wear it, because you had this made just for me.'"

"It *is* beautiful, Neil. And yes, I wish I could wear it. Only you would have had this made just for me."

"Couldn't have said it better myself." He took the ring from the box and held it over her finger. "One final command, Andrea, and we'll get to *your* surprise. But first I must hear you say, 'I know this ring is a symbol of your love and the trust I would never destroy because once I did you'd never trust me again. Please be my husband, and let me be your wife. For now and forever.'"

"Stop it," she cried. "Stop it!"

"Wrong reply. But that was quite a mouthful, so let's make it simple. As in, 'I want to marry you. I want to wear your ring and have your babies.' And you say . . . ?"

"Neil—" She stared from the brutal line of his mouth to the cutting censure in his eyes to the gold-and-diamond promise of a dream. "Neil . . . *may* . . . I?" she sobbed out.

"No, Andrea"—he flung the ring across the room—"you may *not*." Before she could roll off the bed, he pinned her down with his body.

"Let me go. Please, Neil, I'm begging you. Let me go."

"Not on your life. You're not about to throw me off and get away. I do the walking, and I say when."

"You have to listen to me. I can explain. Five minutes, just give me five minutes to make you understand."

"I understand one thing and one thing only." He gripped both her wrists in a single hand. "You lied to me, dammit. *Lied.*"

"I admit it. Okay? I'm guilty. But, Neil, I wasn't—"

"Going to send it?" His mocking laughter filled her ear. "Aw, no no, *chère*, of course not. That's why you hid it from me, right? Now let me guess when you were gonna tell me. Today, I'll just bet."

"Yes! *Yes*, I swear to you. God's truth, I was."

"Uh-huh." His hips brushed a whispered caress over her buttocks. "Sure you were. And I do believe you, *chère*. The same way I believe you haven't already passed the goods on to the highest bidder. How am I doing so far? That was gonna be your next claim to innocence, wasn't it?" When she whimpered, he roared, "*Wasn't it?*"

"Yes. But Neil, it's true. I wrote it only for me. And for you. Not for anyone else. No one's seen it and—"

"Shut up! Shut your lying mouth up and quit insulting me with such predictable tripe. The way it was between us could've been for good if you hadn't ruined us."

"I didn't ruin us, Neil. It's—"

"Too late, that's what it is." He turned her around beneath him, softly kissed her mouth. "You have been a *very* bad girl. Such a bad girl that I want you to beg me to make love to you. And you will. Again. And again. And . . . well, you get the picture. Tonight's the final act, *chère*. We're making it count."

"I loved you, Andrea. God, how I did love you." Neil tenderly stroked a fingertip over her swollen mouth as he studied her tear-streaked face in the midmorning light.

And then he couldn't look at her anymore. If he did, he'd be a bigger sap than the one she'd played him for with a maestro's touch. And all for the sake of a scoop. *Journalists.* How he did hate them. But never more than now.

He got up, feeling her eyes on him. Even with her betrayal ripping him up, he could still feel the heat of hunger her body sparked in him. He was certain it would never go away. Such was the price of a grand passion cut down in its prime by treason.

"If you really loved me, Neil, you would listen to my side of the story."

"And if you'd really loved me, you never would have written one." He turned to her then. "You came for an exclusive, and that's what you got. I've seen the proof. What proof have you got to deny it and convince me your lies *is* God's truth?"

More than anything he wanted her to. He'd give up what was left of his life for a half-baked excuse he could swallow.

Her answer was a pregnant silence, a shuttered stare.

"You got what you came for, Andrea, and I hope you're happy, 'cause I've never been more miserable in my whole miserable life. You've given me one helluva wonderful, wild ride, but this is where I get off. You've got one month to pack your bags and get out. As of now, I'm moving back to my private quarters in the club. If you need more time, call Lou to arrange it. Fair enough?"

"It's not fair at all, Neil. I'll move out today. This is your house, not mine."

"It *was* ours," he said in a battered voice. "We could've had it all if you hadn't violated me. Ever since I found that article, I've felt a certain kinship with rape victims. That's how I feel. *Raped*. Mentally and emotionally violated by a trusted family member. Excuse me while I puke?"

Andrea lunged from the bed after him, but he slammed the bathroom door in her face. She listened to his heaves and muted groans. A flush was followed by the sound of running water. Then the door opened.

"What a final bow, huh?" he said with a bark of laughter. "Thanks for everything—well . . . almost. If a buyer hasn't bitten yet, one's bound to soon. I won't give you my endorsement. But I won't take you to court for it neither. Don't have the stomach for it, *chère*. No more than I do to have whatever the hell you've written made public. I'll pay you for the article. Send me the bill if you so wisely choose and . . . and I need to get out of here."

He turned, and all she could think was that he was walking out of her life, just as he'd walked out on his mass audience. She wasn't only desperate, she was suddenly angry and refusing his refund to a ticket she'd pay for the rest of her life.

"You know what, Slick? You've got a bad habit: quitting. When the world doesn't play by your rules, what do you do? You quit! You're a sore loser, and so you take the easy way out. It's a child's game for a little boy in a man's body. Go ahead and fly. Fly, Peter Pan, *fly*. Take to the air and leave the truth behind you. It's in my drawer that you breached *my* trust by entering."

He swung around at the moment she jerked out the drawer and frantically dug to the bottom. As she waved the papers at him, he came at her and grabbed her wrist.

"Lady, have you got nerve," he bit out. "Get that out of my sight before I tear it up."

"Go ahead, Neil. Tear it up. Quitting doesn't make any of it go away, but like with everything else, you're afraid to deal with it. And do you know what that makes you besides a quitter? A coward. Read it, Neil. I *dare* you." She thrust it at him, and he glared from her to the pages he took from her. "Go ahead and read it. Or don't you have the guts?"

"Anything you've written is something I've told you in confidence. I don't need to read my regurgitated secrets."

"Then why not take it to remember me by?" she taunted him. "Keep the article, read it when I'm gone."

Just when she thought he meant to tear the pages into shreds, he folded the stack over once, twice, and pocketed it.

"How generous. Rest assured I'll put it to good use."

"Then you'll read it?" she asked eagerly.

"In a pig's eye. Christine's off the wall, and I need something to practice on."

"You jerk. You *damn* jerk."

"I've never denied it. But at least I'm an honest jerk. And quite honestly, Andrea, as an artist, I can understand your need to write. We're not so different that way. I hear notes, you hear words, and we put them on paper. And being somewhat ambitious myself, I can even understand what drove you here to get the goods on me. But what I can't understand, and what I *cannot* accept, is that once we shared a bed and I confided in you, you didn't abort your original mission. Look at yourself through my eyes. You are one cold-blooded bitch."

She winced, seeing herself as he did, her mistake for what it was. If only she'd trusted him sooner, she would have told him the tale of a woman who came for a story but ended up with her own happy ending. He might have even laughed, the joke being on her.

Neither was laughing now. She was crying openly, and he looked suspiciously close to joining her.

"I don't suppose there's anything I can say or do to convince you to give me a second chance?"

"As much as I wish there was, no. The trust is gone, and there's no getting it back. Even if we tried to patch ourselves together, it wouldn't be the same. I learned an important lesson from my sorry excuse for a marriage. The loss of trust between two people, whether they love each other or not, is the start of a slow death. Maybe I am a coward, since I'd rather go quick than watch us die slow. What we had was too good. Let's take the memories, *chère*, before we end up destroying them and each other."

But Neil, I'm carrying your baby, she silently wept. How she longed to tell him that, tell him she loved him even now. And yet, could he be right in this? So much damage done. So wrong to bring a child into a relationship devoid of trust. No, she didn't dare tell him of the baby, unless, by some miracle, they could mend. She wiped her eyes and notched up her chin, determined to gather what remained of her dignity.

"Then it's really over."

Neil pulled out his top drawer and withdrew a handkerchief with his initials in red. A present that she'd carefully stitched while they watched *Father Knows Best*. He tenderly stroked her cheeks with the linen, then wiped her nose before placing the hankie in her palm.

"Last time I'll be doin' that, *chère*," he said gruffly. And then sternly added, "This isn't easy for me to say, but it *is* really over. Therefore, you are not to call me. And as of today, you are banned from the club. It's best for us both."

"You sound like that old song, Neil. Cruel to be kind." Damn, why couldn't she quit crying? She had something important to say. Andrea impatiently rubbed her wet cheeks and got it out.

"Even if it's too late for us, it's not too late for you. You have a wonderful gift that you Scrooge away because you're terrified of losing it. And countless others pay the price for your fear. Your money, your rules, they're an illusion of security, the substitutes you cling to because you can't go home. The funny thing is, you've taught me that home can be found in the least-expected places, and it's a lesson you can't grasp yourself. But you could. If you'd only let go of your rage and quit blaming your mother for deserting you."

"She *did* desert me," he insisted angrily.

"No, Neil, she died. *Died*. It wasn't her fault, and it wasn't desertion. Let her go. You can't climb into the casket with her, so forget your rules and join the living."

He shook off her earnest grip on his arm and stalked to the door. There, he turned.

"You and Mama have a lot in common, Andrea. She *did* desert me, as you did in your own way. She didn't have to die any more than you had to kill us. Just as you could've switched your subject, she could have chosen another way out. Mama killed herself. I'm the one that found her. Stayed with her till the neighbors complained about a smell, and the police carted her off. A local newshound shoved a mike under my nose while I hung on to the stretcher. He wanted to know how I felt, why I was clinging to a stiff."

"No," she moaned. "God, *no*."

"Don't tell me you're not impressed. Anything for a story, right? What worked for him certainly served *you*. Anyway, that was my first encounter with a journalist. Left a bad taste in my mouth, though not half as nasty as the one you've given me. Damn juicy copy, *chère*, an exclusive scoop. Not even Lou knows. Stick that in your article for a sure sale."

Seventeen

Twenty days, twenty of the most horrible days of her life, had passed since Neil shut the door. Softly. With the same finality that marked his refusal of her calls, the letters begging for a reconciliation. All sent back unopened.

She couldn't eat. She couldn't sleep. And since she was pregnant, unfortunately she couldn't borrow Neil's old escape in drink. If he looked half as bad as she did, he'd pass for a walking corpse. No amount of concealer could hide the dark circles ringing her eyes.

Wasn't she supposed to be filling out, at least a little? Her clothes hung so loosely, she'd had to dip into her limited savings—*savings* since she was out of a job—to buy a few things that were two sizes smaller.

She was shrinking and so were the few days remaining in the month she had left to live in the empty palace Neil had given her, where they'd made love. Laughed. They'd christened this *their* home. Their now-silent home.

The buzz of electric saws and pounding of nails had ceased the day he left. Not even a roach was there to keep her company. If not for Liza—*thank*

God for Liza—she would be even more isolated than she already was in this mausoleum of memories.

Andrea ground her fists against her eyes as the questions came. Where would she go? How would she support the baby?

Bartending was okay income—at the right place, better than a newspaper wage. But club hours were usually lousy, and writing had become a needling reminder of her misjudgment. No longer a delight, it was a chore.

She couldn't be choosy, not with a baby to support. Andrea clasped her stomach. Tears welled as she looked at her concave belly. Liza had actually said that the mother-to-be was in better shape than the father-who-didn't-know.

What a pair she and Neil made. Two adults victimizing each other with their fears and selfish needs. They were even victimizing their own baby, thanks to their stupid mistakes.

And here she sat pitying herself instead of seeing to the welfare of her child. *Where's your fight, gal?* Andrea was suddenly furious with her own apathy. She clung to that and marched to the closet.

His clothes were still next to hers, and defiantly she tugged off the cashmere cape she should be wearing in New England by now if the tickets she'd found were any indication. Next, she opened her top drawer and took out the jeweler's box.

"Neil, may I?" she gritted out as she opened the top and gazed at the ring. "Guess what, Slick? Maybe you're right, and we'll die a slow death. But for the present, my only concern is making sure this baby lives."

"I'm sorry, Ms. Post, but I have strict orders that you are not allowed in."

"In that case, you've got two choices. Either call the police or get Mr. Grey to this door."

"He's uh . . . uh—he's busy. He won't come."

Andrea gripped the teller's window and commanded herself not to lose control. "In that case, I want to see Lou." Andrea dug into her pocket and extended a bribe she couldn't afford. "Here's a little incentive."

"Keep your money, Ms. Post. I'm glad to get Lou without it."

As she tapped her foot against the concrete sidewalk, Andrea clenched her teeth to stop their chattering. She prayed she wouldn't lose what she carried in her belly if the confrontation with Neil got too ugly.

In a few minutes Lou swung open the glossy black doors and wasted no time in hugging her like the big daddy he was.

"You look like death warmed over, gal."

"You look good to me too, Lou."

"I never felt worse than I do with one look at you. Liza told me you wasn't holdin' up so good. I see she was right."

"Liza's always right. The advice she gave me was the best I could've taken. But I didn't, and it's too late. I need your help, Lou. And by the way, I miss you something awful."

"Same here, but nothing like Slick's missin' you. Lawd, chile, but this is one awful mess, and me and Liza would do anything to help clean it up. Tell me what it is you want."

"Get me in to see Neil. Escort me to his office or wherever he is now. Please, Lou. It's urgent."

"You don't *wanna* see him. Not the way he is now. He ain't been sober in almost a month. He ain't shaved or written a new song either. I seen him bad before, but never like this."

Andrea began to shiver. And then she began to cry. Damn hormones, didn't they realize that people were passing while Lou patted her back? She was still struggling to pull herself together when the entrance door banged open.

"Get off my sidewalk."

Her distress turned to shock. Neil bore no resemblance to the vital man she'd known. His eyes were sunken and glassy, and his hair was uncombed. His shirt and pants were wrinkled. The trademark red suspenders flapped loose by his sides. He looked like a bum. An outraged bum who devoured the sight of her even as he raised his voice to a bellow.

"Did you hear me? Evaporate! Lou, are you leavin' with her or coming inside where you belong?"

"Don't take your anger at me out on Lou, Neil."

"Still preachin' at me, are ya? Save your breath, 'cause any lies you've got to say I don't wanna hear."

Her heart contracted at the sound of his voice, the rough, scratchy voice she hadn't heard in forever. And as long as she could keep him talking, just maybe he'd give in and listen.

"Look at us, Neil, what we've done to each other. We can't go on like this. Please, let me in."

"I let you in once, and you abused the privilege. Now *scram*." He reached into his pocket and thrust a wadded-up tissue into her hand.

The door closed with a swish.

"See what I mean?" Lou picked up the rumpled tissue that had fallen to the sidewalk. "I'll do what I can, but in the state he's in, it ain't much."

Andrea wiped at her cheeks with her forearm while something hard balled up inside her. She needed it, desperately, and she willed the hardness to grow.

"I think you should go in, Lou. Don't worry about me, I'll be okay." She took the ring from her purse and handed it to Lou, who woefully wagged his head. "Would you please give this to Neil? And tell him that I'll be out of the house this time tomorrow."

"But, chile, where will you go?"

"I'm not sure, but even if I were, I wouldn't want Neil to know. I'll call Liza after I get settled. Maybe the two of you can come visit someday. I'd like that. If I could thank Neil for anything, it would be for him sharing you with me."

A single tear rolled down Lou's cheek, and he dabbed it away with the tissue she didn't need anymore. Her own tears had stopped. A sense of calm took hold. Tonight she would eat, pack, and sleep. Tomorrow she'd catch the first plane out—somewhere far away from here.

"Move in with me and Liza," Lou urged. "He won't have to know. After the way he's treated you, he ain't welcome there till he get his head out of his butt, and his mouth off that bottle and onto a cup of coffee."

"Thanks, Lou, but I can't. I have—" She'd almost said that she had to make a clean break for her health and that of the baby. Liza had sworn herself to secrecy, and as much as Andrea wanted to stay, she knew she couldn't survive if she did. "I have to get on with my life. New Orleans has too many memories. I have to leave. I won't be back."

Neil threw a dart at the pages tacked to his office wall, print facing the paint.

The dart speared another tiny hole, speared another memory in his head, one of too many that wouldn't go away no matter how numb he tried to get.

The audience was thinning. He couldn't compose.

He didn't care.

He longed to be dead. And just maybe he would be in another year at the rate he was going. It hurt, Lord yes, it did. But the memories hurt so good that he couldn't let them go, and he lingered in this seductive death.

Neil poised another dart, but before it could fly, the door banged open. Next thing Neil knew, Lou was shaking him by the shirt. Then Lou released him and sent his chair, along with him, smack against the wall.

"Got you somethin', you good-fo'-nothing son of a bitch."

"Don't you ever talk about my mama that way," Neil slurred.

Lou tossed something on his desk, and it landed on the open ledger. Neil stared at the pink heart-shaped diamond. And then he slowly closed the accounting book.

Lou flipped it open, picked up the ring, and shoved it under Neil's gaze.

"Look at it, Slick. Take a good, long look and see what you be throwing away. The best thing you ever had is gone come tomorrow. That is, unless you act quick. Drink some coffee and forget the show. Take yo' ass off this chair and hustle it fast as you can to where it belongs at the only home you've got. Unless you do, you ain't welcome in mine no more."

"Is that all?" Neil demanded, unable to look away from the ring.

"Pretty much. Except I'm givin' you my notice. You got one week to find another pianist or give me a reason to stay. What I'm lookin' at ain't no son of mine or Liza's. You're a disgrace to us and a disgrace to yo' mama, not to mention yo'self. Better hang on to this ring." He slapped it into Neil's palm. "Keep this up, and it won't be long 'fore you need to hock it for another bottle of booze."

Neil was still staring at the ring when he heard the door slam. Dully, he picked up a dart and sent it sailing. The dart fell short of the wall and hit the floor.

He tried to put down the ring, but he couldn't. And so he took it with him as he went to collect his darts. The one on the floor was easy enough, but the ones embedded into the wood weren't so agreeable. A sheet tore at the edge when he yanked out a metal tip, and the corner turned down, the print facing him.

It couldn't get any worse than this, could it? Before he gave himself time to think, he jerked out the darts, one by one, and laid them in a heap on the floor. And then he began to pull out tacks, releasing the pages from the wall. Down they came, one after the other, until his hands were full and the wall was blank but for minuscule holes marring its surface.

"Okay, *chère*, here goes. Make me bleed what little blood you ain't already sucked up and spit out."

Neil forced himself to put the pages in order. And then he forced himself to read the first sentence.

"'There is a gentle cruelty about his mouth,'" he read aloud, "'a cruelty that is kind and generous. He makes us laugh, he makes us weep. He makes us hurt, but the hurt is so good, we beg for more. . . .'" The first paragraph gave way to the second and then the third and then he was turning the page and the page after that. He couldn't stop reading, his eyes feasting on what he was too stunned to completely absorb.

And so he read it again. And again.

He repeated aloud the closing clincher: "'Neil is everything and nothing the public has perceived. He *is* his music—passionate and unpredictable, a devil-may-care joy ride into the darkness of blinding light. The audience is full. The stage is empty. And still the crowd remains rooted in a standing ovation, crying out: "Where did you go? Why did you leave?" as they applaud for an encore.

"'He is an artist shrouded by myth, a musician of incomparable genius. But he's much more than that. A soul who has emerged triumphant over tragedy, a champion of the human spirit. That, as much as his music, defines him. Neil Grey, a man who is every man.

"'A man whose legend is destined to live on long after the curtain closes.'"

After the third reading, Neil pressed the stack of paper to his face. For long minutes he held her words to him, then put them down and went to the door.

"Lou!" he yelled. "Hey, Lou, get yourself in here!"

"What the hell do you want?" Lou growled shortly

after. "Another bottle before you quit cuttin' my checks?"

"Forget the bottle. I want a pot of coffee. Better yet, make it two. And while you're at it, tell the manager there's no cover charge tonight, and to get a fill-in for me."

"Either I need to get my hearing checked or you done asked for a pot of coffee."

"Your hearing's fine. Now test out those eyeballs." Neil pulled the flask from his back pocket and hurled it ten feet into the trash can. "Got you a question, Lou. How do you think this ring looks on my pinkie?" Neil wiggled it back and forth before pressing the stone to his lips.

"Looks like it don't belong there. It'd fit a lot better on a certain woman's hand it was made for."

"Absolutely. Another question. Am I as dumb as I look?"

"Hell, no. You be at least ten times dumber than that."

"*Wrong*, Big Daddy. I've been stupid, real stupid, blind and deaf to boot. But I learn fast when I need to. Did Andrea say where she was headed?"

"Wouldn't say nothing, 'cept she didn't want you to find out. Can you blame her?"

"I don't blame nobody but myself. I've got a date with a razor and the shower. I'd appreciate you bringing me that coffee while I'm at it."

"Two pots of coffee, comin' right up!" Lou gave him a high five and danced his way to the door.

"Daddy?" Neil shucked off his shirt and flung it toward the trash can where his flask was staying for good.

"Yes, Son?"

"Ever since Mama left, I've been lost and done my best to join her in the mist. Andrea blew it away and took me home. If she goes, I'll have to live without even the mist to get lost in, because I see too clearly what I've done. Music's always been a drug for me,

ne I've needed even more than booze. But Andrea,
ne makes them both look like child's play. I need
er, Lou. Even when I hated her for what she'd done,
loved her. I'll always love her. You think there's a
nance she might still be able to love me?"

"I'm the wrong person to ask. The coffee's on its
ay."

As Neil shut the door, the weight of his crime did
attle with hope. *What could he possibly do to make
up to her?*

Eighteen

At first she thought it was the wind whistling outsid
the bedroom window. The sustained crooning be
came louder, then rippled into a cascade of runnin
notes.

Andrea dropped the unfolded blouse into an ope
suitcase on the bed. Though she commanded herse
to shut out the sweet, sinuous sound and to haste
her packing, her ears refused to obey, and so did he
trembling hands.

Only a fool would be seduced by the aching en
treaty from the saxophone below. Only a fool woul
follow the Pied Piper's lure to open the glossy whit
French doors.

Only a fool like her would stand outside on th
wrought iron balcony and fill herself up with th
sight of a man who had wrung her heart dry an
sought to woo it back . . . too late.

He stood on the sidewalk in the moonlight an
continued to play a song she'd never heard. A melod
so poignant that her eyes stung with tears. Sh
blamed it on the cold air, and she told herself th
uncontrollable shaking of her body was due to he
not wearing the coat she'd laid out for tomorrow'
journey.

Her coat. Everything he'd given her she was leav-
g behind. Except for the memories they shared
at swept over her now. As she watched his lips
ake love to the mouthpiece and his fingers stroke
e gold keys, her breasts, so tender of late, felt
avy and full. Her womb quickened and stirred,
sponding as if it were *she* he touched.

Drawing upon the hard core that threatened to
ssolve as she stood there staring down into his
seeching gaze, Andrea shook her head and re-
eated.

When she shut the balcony doors, the music
opped.

Over the raucous beating of her heart she heard
e building's front door close and then the heavy
ead of his steps moving quickly up the stairs. She
antically threw things into her luggage.

"And where the hell do you think you're going with
at?" he demanded, stalking into the bedroom.

"None of your business. As you so eloquently put it
rlier, *scram*."

"Not till you listen to what I've got to say."

"Sorry, Slick, but this time I don't want to hear it.
ou had your chance, and you blew it. Now *blow*."

Andrea decided to take what she had packed and
rget the rest. She clicked the fasteners shut, then
auled the suitcase from the bed. Whirling around,
e collided with his chest. She tried not to notice
at he wore a fresh, starched shirt, that his stern
ce was nicked but cleanly shaven, and that the
ench of his fingers over hers generated a too-
miliar sizzle.

Jerking her hand away, she belatedly realized that
allowed him to claim the luggage. He sent it
idding across the room, then caught her shoulders
ith a firm, caressing grip.

"Wanna slap me? Take your best shot and make it
unt. I don't intend to offer ever again."

"No thanks, I've already expended too much energy

on you. As for any future rights to slug you, we hav
no future."

"Why not? Because you don't want to marry a
idiot who betrayed *your* trust by refusing to liste
when he should have believed in you and forgotte
his stupid damn rules?"

They were stupid rules, but surely no more stupi
than she was, standing there, soaking up his touch
and eagerly listening to his every word when sh
should be clamping her hands over her ears an
dashing for the door.

"I think that sums it up pretty well," she said
making an effort to keep her voice icy while sh
warmed to his.

"No *chère*, that's not half the tally of my sin
against you. Any mistakes you made can't compar
with mine."

"I'm glad you realize that. I suppose you read m
article?"

"I did. Felt like I had my teeth kicked in and m
brain jarred loose. I've done terrible damage to you
to us. Everything you ever accused me of is true—
ducking out when I can't call the shots, leaving m
messes behind for someone else to clean up. Tryin
to run home to a mother who's dead and gone whe
my home was here with you all along. How you eve
loved me is beyond my limited comprehension."

"It's not necessarily limited," she said hesitantly
"Let's just say extremely slow."

"I am truly a terrible man," he said, kissing he
palm. "Not a boy, not anymore, Andrea. I'm pleadin
with you to believe that the boy's been laid to res
with his mama and a man's come home to tell yo
he's learned from his mistakes, that he wants t
spend the rest of his life making it up to you. Startin
now. I made a couple of calls before I came here. On
was to an editor I promised a copy of your articl
to. Good thing he was working late, and I hadn'
thrown away his business card. We're not exactl

good buds, but he does give me a call every now and then with a standing invitation to do an interview. I could hear him salivating on the other end when I made him a deal that was sweeter than a praline. Heard enough? Or would you care to know the deal?"

"You—you actually called an editor on my behalf?" Who cared about the deal? she thought, trying to temper her joy. She didn't even care if her words made it to print.

"Not only that, I negotiated the fee while I was at it. Hope you don't mind. I got him to pay you not for one piece, but two. There's some big news in the recording world I guaranteed him an exclusive to—with the understanding that you cover the assignment."

"Exclusive . . . assignment . . . ?" She was dizzy, clutching at his arms for support, and he scooped her up and sat on the bed's edge, holding her so tightly, so close, that his voice was muffled against her neck.

"That's right. Complete with a photo shoot and the story behind the songs I'm scheduled to record on an independent label. Just so happens I've got a musician friend who went into that end of the business last year. He's struggling to get a foothold, but he's honest and flying right high since we reached a gentleman's agreement on the phone. Soon as we hung up, I ran over here fast as I could. Felt like I'd smoked a carton. I've been going through more than two a week. Hear me out and I'll quit, cold turkey."

Neil, willing to give up one of his fondest vices? He *was* desperate. As desperate as she. A few minutes of her listening time could add years to his life. And—sweet heaven, could it be?—years to a lifetime together.

"I'm listening."

"Okay, here goes. It's not a standard contract. I didn't want any up-front money or royalties. Instead, I get a share of his company—in your name and mine. Plus, I get complete artistic control. Cover art included."

"That's wonderful, Neil, that's—I can't believe this."

"Believe it. Guess whose picture'll be on the cover?"

"Yours?"

"Guess again. The album's entitled *Andrea*. You did inspire every note. Only problem is, you inspired me so much, I've got enough compositions for three releases. My professional judgment tells me they'll do real well. It is my best work. Could be I'll have to do some promotion, travel a bit. If I've managed to convince you not to leave me, could I maybe talk you into keeping me company if I have to go on the road from time to time? Save your money, and let me buy you a portable computer to cover the action. 'Fraid it won't be the juiciest copy. Not since I'm cleaning up my act."

"No—no public scenes?"

"The one in front of the club was my last. Adults do prefer to settle disputes in private."

"What about your flask?"

"Trashed. Gone for good. My days of drinking alone or to excess are hereby over. I vow it on my mother's grave. The only exception I'll make is if you're ever in the mood to trade body shots—alone. But even then not to excess." His hand glided over her leg and massaged the interior of her thigh, which quivered in a quick response. "*Especially* not then. I don't want to be numb. Not now and never again. What you make me feel, what we've got, it's too special."

"But, Neil," she said shakily, "there can't be any body shots tonight."

"What are you saying, that you want some time to think all this over? That you won't put this on?" He pulled the ring off his pinky and held it over her finger where it had belonged from the beginning, where it was meant to be forever.

"What I'm saying is . . . how do you feel about
ody shots with seltzer water?"

"Seltzer water never tasted better, just so the body
m kissin' is yours. Even if it does feel awful skinny.
did this to you, *chère*, turned you into a bunch of skin
nd bones. Forgive me. Please forgive me, 'cause I
an't forgive myself."

She released the buttons running the length of his
hirt and pressed a lingering kiss to his chest.

"Make you a deal, Slick. But you must obey the
ules."

"Lay 'em out and I'll abide by them till death do us
art."

"In that case . . . First, I need to hear you say
hat you love me."

"Hell yes, I love you. I love you more than my
nusic, more than any of my dumb rules or even
lumber vices, Andrea. You're the only woman I've
ver loved, and I swear I'll never love another."

"Very good," she murmured, and wiggled her ring
inger. "Second, I would like you to propose. No 'kind
f' proposal and no head games."

Neil's steady gaze held hers as he said somberly,
Andrea, will you marry me, for better or worse,
specially if I promise to be the best damn husband
ou could ever have?"

"I will."

"Then *may* I place this ring on your finger?"

"Yes, Neil, you may."

She watched as the diamond heart slid down the
apered length, and she felt the warm, smooth circle
f gold come to rest in a secure fit. Neil bowed his
ead and sealed the binding vow with a kiss.

Andrea urged his head lower until she pressed it to
er abdomen. "Third," she said a little breathlessly,
scarcely able to contain her joy, "how do you feel
bout factoring and multiplying two halves that
nake each other whole? That's probably not a logical

math theory, but we do have a new equation. You
know, one plus one makes three?"

Neil stilled, and then he was suddenly pressing her
down deep into the mattress, his face eager and
hopeful and anxious and hovering over hers.

"*Chère,* you're not telling me that—"

"Four was always my lucky number too, Neil. So
maybe there's a chance we'll have twins. I'd like to
seal the deal with a kiss to make up for the ones
we've lost."

He possessively caressed her belly while he claimed
her mouth in a searing reunion. A hungry kiss, a
mad mating of lips, full of passion and fire.

"Make love with me, *chère.* I want to make love like
we've never made it before," he whispered fiercely as
his hands roved over her. "This won't do. It won't do
atall. After we tear up the sheets, you're gettin' some
rest while I make the best jambalaya you ever ate.
I'm fattening you up."

"I'd really like that. But I won't cooperate unless
you share my bowl." She stroked the shadowed
hollows of his cheeks, and her voice choked. "You
look like hell."

"I've never felt so close to heaven. What-say we top
the night off with *beignets,* then meet Lou and Liza at
the airport? We'll take the first nonstop flight to
Vegas, then head for a honeymoon in New England
before you come to your senses. Are you game?"

"On one condition."

"Name it, Mrs. Grey. A dime a dance or a quarter a
song, it's yours, and I'm gladly payin'. Hmmm. Great
titles. 'Dime a Dance.' 'Quarter a Song.' 'It's Yours
and I'm Gladly Paying.' You mind if I compose some
on our honeymoon? Seems Simon's makin' a curtain
call."

"Tell Simon that you're busy and you'll catch him
later."

"Done. So what's the condition?"

"Before you fatten me up and hustle us all to the airport, I'd like to watch *Father Knows Best*."

"Hush," he growled against her belly. "We've got plenty of time to make our own home movies that'll outshine any old reruns, 'cause they'll be ours and they'll be real. Trust me, *chère*. Just like I should've always trusted you, and from here on I will, no question. I might be a slow learner, but the lessons I learn do stick."

As he kissed his way down, she sifted her fingers through his hair and sighed happily. "It would seem that tonight Father *does* know best."

THE EDITOR'S CORNER

oon we'll be rushing into the holiday season, and we have ome special LOVESWEPT books to bring you good cheer. othing can put you in a merrier mood than the six fabulous mances coming your way next month.

he first book in our lineup is **PRIVATE LESSONS** by arbara Boswell, LOVESWEPT #582. Biology teacher Gray IcCall remembers the high school student who'd had a ush on him, but now Elissa Emory is all grown up and uite a knockout. Since losing his family years ago, he adn't teased or flirted with a woman, but he can't resist hen Elissa challenges him to a sizzling duel of heated mbraces and fiery kisses. Extracurricular activity has never een as tempting as it is in Barbara's vibrantly written mance.

/ith **THE EDGE OF PARADISE,** LOVESWEPT #583, eggy Webb will tug at your heartstrings—and her hero will apture your heart. David Kelly is a loner, a man on the run ho's come looking for sanctuary in a quiet Southern town. till, he can't hide his curiosity—or yearning—for the lovely oman who lives next door. When he feels the ecstasy of eing in Rosalie Brown's arms, he begins to wonder if he as left trouble behind and finally found paradise. A superb ve story from Peggy!

nly Jan Hudson can come up with a heroine whose ability accurately predict the weather stems from her once aving been struck by lightning! And you can read all about in **SUNNY SAYS,** LOVESWEPT #584. Kale Hoaglin is ceptical of Sunny Larkin's talent, and that's a problem since e's the new owner of the small TV station where Sunny works as the weather reporter. But her unerring predictions—and thrilling kisses—soon make a believer of him. Jan continues to delight with her special blend of love and laughter.

Please give a rousing welcome to new author Debora Harmse and her first novel, **A MAN TO BELIEVE IN**, LOVESWEPT #585. This terrific story begins when Cori McLaughlin attends a costume party and catches the eye of a wickedly good-looking pirate. Jake Tanner can mesmerize any woman, and Cori's determined not to fall under his spell. But to be the man in her life, Jake is ready to woo her with patience, persistence, and passion. Enjoy one of our New Faces of 1992!

Michael Knight feels as if he's been **STRUCK BY LIGHT NING** when he first sees Cassidy Harrold, in LOVESWEPT #586 by Patt Bucheister. A mysterious plot of his matchmaking father brought him to England, and with one glimpse of Cassidy, he knows he'll be staying around for a while. Cassidy has always had a secret yen for handsome cowboys, and tangling with the ex–rodeo star is wildly exciting, but can she be reckless enough to leave London behind for his Montana home? Don't miss this enthralling story from Patt!

Tonya Wood returns to LOVESWEPT with **SNEAK**, #587, and this wonderful romance has definitely been worth waiting for. When Nicki Sharman attacks the intruder in her apartment, she thinks he's an infamous cat burglar. But he turns out to be Val Santisi, the rowdy bad boy she's adored since childhood. He's working undercover to chase a jewel thief, and together they solve the mystery of who's robbing the rich—and steal each other's heart in the process. Welcome back, Tonya!

FANFARE presents four spectacular novels that are on sale this month. Ciji Ware, the acclaimed author of *Romantic Times* award-winner **ISLAND OF THE SWANS**, delivers

WICKED COMPANY, an engrossing love story set in London during the eighteenth century. As Sophie McGann moves through the fascinating—and bawdy—world of Drury Lane, she remains loyal to her dream . . . and the only man she has ever loved.

Trouble runs deep in **STILL WATERS,** a novel of gripping suspense and sensual romance by Tami Hoag, highly praised author of **LUCKY'S LADY.** When the body of a murder victim literally falls at Elizabeth Stuart's feet, she's branded a suspect. But Sheriff Dane Jantzen soon becomes convinced of her innocence, and together they must find the killer before another deadly strike can cost them their chance for love, even her very life.

In the grand tradition of **THORN BIRDS** comes **THE DREAMTIME LEGACY** by Norma Martyn, an epic novel of Australia and one unforgettable woman. Jenny Garnett is indomitable as she travels through life, from a childhood in a penal colony to her marriage to a mysterious aristocrat, from the harshness of aching poverty to the splendor of unthinkable riches.

Treat yourself to **MORE THAN FRIENDS,** the classic romance by bestselling author BJ James. In this charming novel, corporate magnate John Michael Bradford meets his match when he's rescued from a freak accident by diminutive beauty Jamie Brent. Mike always gets what he wants, and what he wants is Jamie. But growing up with six brothers has taught independent Jamie never to surrender to a man who insists on always being in control.

Also on sale this month in the hardcover edition from Doubleday is **LAST SUMMER** by Theresa Weir. The author of **FOREVER** has penned yet another passionate and emotionally moving tale, one that brings together a bad-boy actor and the beautiful widow who tames his heart.

The Delaneys are coming next month from FANFARE! This legendary family's saga continues with **THE DELANEY CHRISTMAS CAROL,** three original and sparkling novellas by none other than Iris Johansen, Kay Hooper, and Fayrene Preston. Read about three generations of Delaneys in love and the changing faces of Christmas past, present, and future—only from FANFARE.

Happy reading!

With best wishes,

Nita Taublib
Associate Publisher
LOVESWEPT and FANFARE

Don't miss these fabulous Bantam Fanfare
titles on sale in OCTOBER.

WICKED COMPANY
by Ciji Ware

STILL WATERS
by Tami Hoag

THE DREAMTIME LEGACY
by Norma Martyn

MORE THAN FRIENDS
by BJ James

And in hardcover from Doubleday,
LAST SUMMER
by Theresa Weir

WICKED COMPANY
by Ciji Ware
the bestselling author of
ISLAND OF THE SWANS

Eighteenth-century Scotland is a man's world, and a woman has few rights. But when Sophie McGann's father dies in prison after angering a powerful aristocrat, Sophie learns to fight for herself. Looking for a new start, she takes on the glorious and bawdy world of London's Drury Lane in the golden age of British theatre. There she becomes a favorite of the brilliant theatre manager David Garrick, who encourages Sophie's skill as a playwright. But Sophie also attracts the attention of dangerous men: a rigid censor who can destroy her career; a charming young wastrel who will try to maneuver her into marriage; an enigmatic nobleman who wants to possess her. Through it all Sophie remains loyal to the writer's fire that burns within her, and to the only man she loves, the Scottish actor Hunter Robertson—even when all she holds dear is at risk.

STILL WATERS
by Tami Hoag
"A master of the genre" —*Publisher's Weekly*

"Tami Hoag belongs at the top of everyone's favorite author list."
—*Romantic Times*

**A sizzling novel of romantic suspense by the author of
LUCKY'S LADY.**

All Elizabeth Stuart wants is a chance to reclaim her peace of mind—to escape the memories of a painful divorce. But she quickly discovers that in a small town called Still Creek, trouble is around every bend. For one day a murder victim literally falls at her feet, branding her a suspect and *bringing her under the searching gaze of local sheriff Dane Jantzen. In the following scene, which begins at the site of the crime, Dane has all but accused her of the murder, and Elizabeth is having more than a little trouble restraining her temper. . . .*

"At a loss for words, Ms. Stuart?" he asked softly, arching a mocking brow.

"No," she said through clenched teeth, her furious gaze fastening to the open neck of his black polo shirt because she didn't think she could look him in the eye without losing her temper altogether. "I just can't seem to find one bad enough to call you."

"There's a thesaurus on my desk. Feel free to use it."

"Don't tempt me, sugar," she said, lifting her chin and fixing him with a glare as she took a step back toward the waiting deputy. "What I'd like to do with it wouldn't exactly be good for the binding."

Dane chuckled in spite of the fact that he disliked her. She had a lot of sass . . . and a backside that could make a man's palms sweat, he observed as she sauntered away with Ellstrom. The way she filled out a pair of jeans was enough to make Levi Strauss rise from the dead. He felt his own body stir in response and he frowned.

It was too damn bad there was a chance she was a killer.

"You had better wait in the sheriff's office." The dispatcher hustled her into the office, thrust a Styrofoam cup of black coffee into her hand and bolted for her station, swinging the door shut behind her. That effectively cut the noise level erupting in the room beyond to a dull buzz, enclosing Elizabeth in a cocoon of peace.

To distract herself, she began a tour of the sheriff's office, studying, looking for clues about the man. Not that she cared on a personal level, she reminded herself. From what she'd seen, Dane Jantzen was a Grade A bastard. It was just good sense to know your adversary. She'd learned that lesson the hard way, underestimating her ex-husband's power and ruthlessness. Besides, she wanted every detail she could get for her story. She was a journalist now, albeit at a podunk weekly newspaper in

Middle of Nowhere, Minnesota, but a journalist nevertheless, and she was determined to do the job right.

She glanced around the office. There was nothing here of Dane Jantzen the man, no mounted deer heads or bowling trophies.

He was neat. Not a good sign. Men who were neat liked to be in control of everything and everyone around them. Dane Jantzen's desk shouted control. Files were labeled, stacked, and lined up just so. His blotter was spotless. His pens were all in their little ceramic holder, tips down.

Beside the telephone was the one personal item in the room—a small wooden picture frame. Dangling her cigarette from her lip, Elizabeth lifted the frame and turned it for a look. The photograph was of a young girl, perhaps ten or eleven, just showing signs of growing into gangly youth. Dressed in baggy shorts and a blazing orange T-shirt, she stood on a lawn somewhere holding up a sign done in multi-colored Magic Markers that read "I love you, Daddy."

Elizabeth felt a jolt of surprise and something else. *Daddy.* She took a drag on her cigarette and exhaled a jet stream of blue smoke as she returned the picture to its place.

"Jesus," she muttered. "Someone actually married the son of a bitch."

"She has since seen the error of her ways, I assure you," Dane said dryly.

Elizabeth whirled, managing to look guilty and knock her coffee to the floor all at once.

"Shit! I'm sorry."

He stuck his head out into the hall and calmly called to the dispatcher. "Lorraine, could we get a couple of towels in here, please?"

"I was looking for an ashtray," Elizabeth said, not quite able to meet Jantzen's steady gaze. She stooped down and grabbed the cup, dabbing ineffectually at the stain on the rug with a wadded-up Kleenex she'd fished out of the pocket of her jeans.

"I don't smoke." He hitched at his jeans and hunkered down in front of her. "It's not good for you."

Elizabeth forced a wry laugh, dousing the stub of her cigarette in what coffee was left in the cup. "What is these days besides oat bran and abstinence?"

"Telling the truth, for starters," Dane said placidly.

She lifted her head and sucked in a gulp of air, startled by his nearness. He was staring at her with those cool unblinking blue eyes. The corners of the sensually curved mouth curled up slightly in that predatory way. He made no move to touch her, but she could feel him just the same. He was too close.

Instinctively she leaned back, but her fanny hit the front of his desk and she realized he had her trapped. It wasn't a pleasant sensation. Neither was the strange racing of her heart. This was hardly the time for her hormones to kick in. Fighting the feelings, she lifted her stubborn chin and looked him in the eye.

"Telling the truth is my business, sheriff."

"Really? I thought you were a reporter."

The gray eyes flashed like lightning behind storm clouds. Dane smiled a little wider and leaned a little closer, driven to recklessness by something he didn't quite understand. He enjoyed baiting her. He put the rush down to the excitement of the game, even though deep down he knew there were sexual connotations that had certainly been missing when he'd relished a win on the football field. This was a different kind of game. Elizabeth Stuart was a beautiful woman. He wasn't stupid enough to get involved with her, but that didn't mean he couldn't skirt the edges a little bit. It was like teasing an animal in a cage—he was safe just as long as he stayed back far enough to keep from getting bitten.

At that thought, his gaze drifted to her mouth. Cherry red. Cherry ripe. Too damn close.

"Your towels, sheriff."

Lorraine's stern, disapproving voice broke the sexual tension. Dane pushed himself to his feet and took the terry cloths the dispatcher thrust at him.

"Thank you, Lorraine."

"I've told those people out there you have nothing further to say, but they aren't leaving. Apparently they're waiting for *her*," she said, stabbing Elizabeth with a pointed look.

Elizabeth rose on shaky legs, setting aside the coffee cup with one hand and raking back her wild black mane with the other. "I won't have anything to say to them."

"Have Ellstrom roust them out of here," Dane said. "They can wait in the parking lot."

The secretary nodded and went to do his bidding. Dane dropped the towels to the wet spot on the floor and stepped on them with the toe of his sneaker. He glanced up at Elizabeth from beneath his eyelashes.

"Is your refusal to talk to them just professional courtesy or are you more concerned about the anything-you-say-can-and-will-be-used-against-you-in-a-court-of-law thing?"

"Why should I be worried about that? You haven't charged me with anything. Or is that your cute little way of telling me you've decided I killed Jarvis, then obligingly called 911? Please, Sheriff, I hope I don't look that stupid."

"Naw . . . stupid isn't how you look at all," he drawled, sliding into the chair behind his desk. He let his gaze glide down her, from the top of her tousled head down to the wet spot on the knee of her tight jeans where the coffee had got her on its way to the floor.

He was being an asshole and he knew it, but he couldn't seem to help himself. Elizabeth Stuart was just the kind of woman who brought out the bastard in him—beautiful, ambitious, greedy, willing to use herself to get what she wanted, willing to use anyone she knew. His gaze drifted back up and lingered on the swell of her breasts.

"Christ, you ought to about have it all memorized by now, hadn't you?" Elizabeth snapped, dropping her hands to her hips. It unnerved her to have him look at her that way. It unnerved her even more to feel excitement sparking to life inside her. It made her wonder if her body didn't just have fatally bad judgment in men. This one was six lanky feet of trouble, and logically she knew better than to get within scratching distance of him, but logic couldn't explain the heat his gaze inspired, nor could it dispel the disappointment she felt in herself for being attracted to him.

He didn't apologize for his rudeness. She doubted he ever apologized for anything. He nodded toward the visitor's chair in a silent order for her to sit, the gesture once again reminding her of a Nordic prince. He sat in his desk chair with a kind of negligent grace, staring at her with his brooding blue eyes. Jantzen didn't seem a particularly Scandinavian name. The Z made her think it was probably Slavic. But the blood was there somewhere, maybe on his mother's side—if he had one, she added uncharitably. The sleek blond hair, the high broad forehead, the heavy brow, the unyielding jaw, those cool, cool eyes all spoke of some kinship with the Vikings.

He nodded again toward the chair. "Have a seat, Mrs. Stuart."

"Miss," she corrected him, moving her camera from the chair to a stack of files on the desk. She settled herself on the chair and pulled her purse onto her lap to hunt for another cigarette.

"You dropped the Mrs., but kept the last name. Is that proper?"

"I don't really give a damn."

"I suppose by that point in time you'd probably lost track of what name to go back to anyway."

That wasn't true, but Elizabeth didn't tell Dane Jantzen. Her roots went back to West Texas, scenic rock and rattlesnake country, to a cowboy named J.C. Shelby and a mother who had died before Elizabeth could store any memories of her. But that was all too personal to reveal to this man.

Under the cynical hide she had grown over the years there was too much vulnerability. She seldom acknowledged it, but she knew it was there. She would have to be a fool to reveal it to this man, and she had ceased being a fool some time ago. So she let Dane Jantzen think what he wanted and told herself his sarcasm couldn't hurt her.

"I can see where you might have felt you didn't get anything out of him in the divorce so you might as well try to wring a few bucks out of his name," Jantzen said, steepling his long fingers in front of him. "That's just business as usual for you, right?"

"I kept the name because my son didn't need another change in his life," she said, her cool snapping like a dry twig beneath the weight of the sheriff's taunt. She leaned forward on her chair, poised for battle, shaking her cigarette at him. "He didn't need another reminder that Brock Stuart didn't want him."

And neither did I.

The words hung in the air between them, unspoken but adding to the thick emotional tension. Dane sat back, a little shaken, a little ashamed of himself, not at all pleased that his poking had stripped away a layer of armor and given him a glimpse of the woman behind it. The truth was he didn't want

Elizabeth Stuart to be anything other than what he had preconceived her to be—a cold, calculating, manipulative gold digger.

Elizabeth sat back, forcing her stiff shoulders against the chair, a little shaken, a lot afraid that she had just revealed a weakness. What had happened to her restraint? What had happened to that hard-earned thick skin? The stress of the evening was wearing on her. And Dane Jantzen was wearing on her. To cover her blunder she turned the cigarette in her hand, planted it between her lips and lit it as quickly as she could so as not to let Jantzen see her hands shake.

"I'd rather you didn't smoke," he said.

"And I'd rather you weren't a jerk." She deliberately took a deep pull on the cigarette, presented him with her profile and fired a stream of smoke into the air, looking askance at him. "Looks like neither one of us is going to get our wish."

Dane yanked open a desk drawer, pulled out a black plastic ashtray and tossed it across the desk in her general direction.

Elizabeth arched a brow. "What a gentleman."

"You ought to see what they taught me in charm school."

THE DREAMTIME LEGACY
by bestselling Australian author
Norma Martyn

In the tradition of THE THORN BIRDS, THE DREAMTIME LEGACY is a magnificent, epic novel of Australia and the unforgettable woman who tames this harsh, beautiful land and makes it her own.

From her childhood in the gutters of an Aussie penal colony to her marriage at the age of eleven to a mysterious English aristocrat, from aching poverty to unimaginable riches, Jenny Garnett is a woman of indomitable strength and courage. Set against the fascinating, exotic, little-known heart of Australia, THE DREAMTIME LEGACY brings to life the legendary outback—and a heroine as fiery as Scarlett O'Hara.

Travis was waiting for Jenny when she left the tavern.

She glanced at him, her eyes narrowing, and began to run toward the waterfront lodgings of the serving girls.

"Wait!" he called to her. "You have no need to run away. I merely wish to speak with you."

She paused, turning toward him, watching him approach.

"What do you want to talk to me about?"

When he asked her to marry him, she stared at him, eyes again wary.

"Don't you trust me?" he asked, studying her in the light of the oil lamps along the waterfront.

"You're crazed," she said slowly, still watching him cautiously, her hands beginning to curl into two balled fists, readying to protect her.

"Do I look crazed?"

"No. But you talk crazed."

"Because I asked you to marry me?" When she did not reply, he continued patiently, "I came to Sydney to find a wife. When I saw you, I decided you would fill the role quite adequately. What I mean is, I decided you would fill the bill. Do you understand?"

She stared at him a moment longer, then nodded.

"Well now. We're making progress," Travis said. "In this Colony it's not unusual for a man to visit Sydney to select a wife from among the women he notices, is it?"

"I don't know."

"How long have you been in the Colony?"

"Always."

"Then you must know," he said, impatience edging into his voice. "It's common practice here. It happens all the time."

"Not to me, it doesn't!" Jenny retorted, responding to the changed tone of his voice.

"You're not already married, are you?" he asked.

She laughed then, and shook her head.

"Do you have parents I should consult? Your mother or your father?"

"My mother's dead." She frowned, then added, "My father's gone too."

A thought occurred to Travis. "Are you an indentured servant in the tavern? A convict?"

She shook her head again.

"Then you're quite free?"

She nodded, remembering the birds, and she smiled at him or the first time.

"That's better. You're not very talkative . . . an advantage n the wife a man chooses."

"Did you really choose me?" she asked. "You weren't just alking crazed? Or funning me?"

"I don't have time to make sport of finding a wife," he replied hortly. "I want to leave the Colony tomorrow. I need to return 1ome." He paused for a moment, looking out toward the head-ands and the open ocean beyond. "We have a long journey outh and we need to complete the journey before the early nows arrive."

"Snow?" Jenny looked at him, her eyes widening. "I've never een snow. But I know what snow is." She smiled at him again, ι show of pride in her expression reflecting the spirit he had detected earlier. "I can read and write. Now I'm up to reading a 2ook. A whole book! That's how I learned about snow."

"You'll learn more about it where we're going."

"Where are you taking me?"

"A long way. High up into the Australian alps. To a valley :here."

"Are there birds where you're taking me?"

"Many birds. And many animals too."

"I'd like to go with you if there are birds there."

"Then that's settled. We can be married tonight," he told her. "I've already made the arrangements."

Everything in its proper order, he thought. Back to front and upside down, like the country he now chose to call home. First the saddle ordered, then the mare selected. First the preacher arranged, then the wife selected.

He stared at the harbor for a while, then toward the open ocean beyond.

The girl watched him, a somber older wisdom slowly shadow-ing her young face.

"You're an English gentleman," she said finally. "I can tell by the way you talk. Not from the things you say but by the way you say them." There was the beginning of retreat in her voice, and of regret on her face. "You choosed me 'cause you thought I was a respectable serving wench. But I'm convict blood, mother and father both. You asked me about them but I didn't properly tell you. My mother was a half-starved foundling to begin with and a thief and a whore all her life. And I've no way of knowing who my father was, though she did say he was likely one of two either a Cockney cut-throat who got himself hanged before was born or one of the Irish rebels she spent a spell with. I've always felt in myself it was an Irish convict and not the other one."

She was watching him as she spoke. When he turned to look at her, her determination faltered.

"You're talkative when you choose to be," he said.

"I'm a good girl for all my bad blood," she told him then. "But it's best you know all that, so you can have second thoughts."

She waited for him to speak—a brown-haired waif with merry green eyes that had become serious, asking for nothing, expecting nothing.

"One of these days, when we've been married for a while and we know each other better, I may tell you about myself," Travis said.

One of these days. But he knew he never would. And he felt certain he would never be questioned by Jenny Garnett.

He no longer questioned himself. There came a time when a man couldn't stomach the half-truths he told others; even less the half-truths he told himself. Then he shut a door on questions and answers, and built whatever he could on whatever was left.

"There's one thing I think you should tell me about yourself before then," Jenny said.

Her words cut so sharply across his thoughts, he glared at her.

"What do you feel you have a right to know?" he demanded, his tone rough and harsh.

"Just one thing, sir. What's your name?"

Travis burst into laughter, a strident sound abrasive to his own ears.

"Jonathan Travis," he told her; and he laughed again at the bitter half-truth even in that.

MORE THAN FRIENDS
by BJ James

His hands stopped their stroking and untangled from her hair to frame her face. Slowly his head descended to hers. There was no urgency, no deep, frantic need, only the sweet kiss of promise. When he lifted his lips from hers, Jamie could only think of this moment, this instant. There were no frustrations, no anger, no troublesome reporters, and no disillusioning mistakes in the past. There was only Mike.

Because of her intense training schedule, Jamie had never learned to hide her response behind a cloak of flirtatiousness. Those teen years when most girls were perfecting the art, she had spent perfecting her gymnastics skills. She had never been anything but straightforward and totally honest. That beguiling truthfulness was a window to her heart.

She feared the experienced man who was now towering over her could read every thought that was sure to be written on her expressive face. Even now he was watching her silently, holding her gently, as she ran the gamut from elation to panic. Despite

her efforts at control, her delicate brows arched up in wonde
her sapphire eyes sparkled in excitement, the soft and tend
curve of her lips trembled on the brink of a smile. Then, just
swiftly, the smile faded, even as it was born. A shiver passe
through her as a shutter came down over the glow in her fac
Instantly her guard was up. She could feel his piercing gaze
she struggled valiantly to gather her scattered thoughts, t
become again the coolly aloof Jamie. Jamie, who cloaked herse
in aloneness. Now she felt the small crack that had appeared i
her wall of defense, and she must begin to mend it, while she sti
could. The battle he had predicted had begun, and Jamie kne
she was fighting herself as well as Mike.

Wisely he put her from him. The faintly mocking smile tha
marked his face was for himself, not the sweet innocent wh
could devastate him with her eyes. When he spoke, there was n
mockery or teasing, only gentle caring.

"Tonight, whether you admit it or not, that shield you'v
been hiding behind has cracked. I serve you fair warning: I'll us
any means to keep the rift open until someday you help me tea
it away."

"I won't."

"You will, but don't be frightened. I might not be fair, but
will be gentle, I will be patient, and I will win." He touched he
cheek softly, his voice even huskier. "I've never before been
patient lover, but never before was there a Jamie Brent."

"This is impossible," she whispered.

"No, honey, it's inevitable."

Jamie shivered beneath his certainty. With her once gleam
ing eyes grown dark, she reached for the pins that had held he
hair. She felt the need to control the tangled locks as she woul
her capricious emotions.

"No," he growled, capturing her hand in his as it hovere
over the low table where he had dropped the pins. "Leave i
down. I like it free."

"Very well, if you wish." She could feel his anger at her nee
to withdraw behind her wall of total control for it grated in hi
voice. With stilted gestures she used her free hand to push he
hair back from her shoulders. It fell gloriously, shining and
healthy, to her waist. "If you still insist we go out to dinne
dressed as we are, I suggest we leave now."

"Jamie"—he caught her other hand—"don't shut me out. The woman who opened the door to me tonight was alive and full of joy. Don't lock her away. She'll die, honey. She'll die without ever having lived. Let her be free and as vibrantly alive as she can be. Don't twist all your emotions into a tight little not until they wither and die." He wound a strand of hair round his hand. "Don't confine her hair, or her spirit. Be a woman. Entrance me, beguile me, tease me as you did tonight with those marvelous clothes. For a moment I saw a woman who could conquer the world with her smile.

"Come out from behind that protective cloak that has kept you an innocent." He paused at the harsh hiss of her indrawn breath. "No, don't deny it. In many ways you're the most innocent twenty-six-year-old woman I've ever seen. Innocent in the ways of women, innocent of your strength. Come into the real world, stand on your own two feet, ply your womanly wiles. Flaunt your charms, flex your wings, and learn the power you can wield. Jamie, Jamie, you could drive a man to the brink of madness."

"You're crazy. I can't do that. I wouldn't know how."

"Then learn, and begin with me. First, last, and always."

She watched his solemn face for a long while. "You're serious, aren't you?"

"Never more."

"I don't understand. Why should you bother? Why should you care?"

"It's simple. I want you to come to me as all the woman you can be. I want the fire and I want the excitement only you can give me. Ours could be an explosive relationship. We could share a matchless love, but only if each of us brings total commitment to our joining. I'm selfish, honey; I want it all. I want the woman in my life to love me without reservations—as I'll love her."

"Mike, you're going too fast for me. All the other was fun and games compared to this. I'm not ready for it. I'm not sure I'll ever be."

"I hadn't intended getting into this tonight. You're right, it's far too soon. Let's forget it for now. I'm still starved."

Jamie burst into hearty laughter that was tinged with relief. "I suppose giants do need to refuel with a certain regularity. Come you poor man, let's go."

Though an easy rapport had been established, she was still wary and was likely to be for some time. But the crack was still there in the wall. It was a beginning.

OFFICIAL RULES TO WINNERS CLASSIC SWEEPSTAKES

No Purchase necessary. To enter the sweepstakes follow instructions found elsewhere in this offer. You can also enter the sweepstakes by hand printing your name, address, city, state and zip code on a 3" x 5" piece of paper and mailing it to: Winners Classic Sweepstakes, P.O. Box 785, Gibbstown, NJ 08027. Mail each entry separately. Sweepstakes begins 12/1/91. Entries must be received by 6/1/93. Some presentations of this sweepstakes may feature a deadline for the Early Bird Prize. If the offer you receive does, then to be eligible for the Early Bird prize your entry must be received according to the Early Bird date specified. Not responsible for lost, late, damaged, misdirected, illegible or postage due mail. Mechanically reproduced entries are not eligible. All entries become property of the sponsor and will not be returned.

Prize Selection/Validations: Winners will be selected in random drawings on or about 7/30/93, by VENTURA ASSOCIATES, INC., an independent judging organization whose decisions are final. Odds of winning are determined by total number of entries received. Circulation of this sweepstakes is estimated not to exceed 200 million. Entrants need not be present to win. All prizes are guaranteed to be awarded and delivered to winners. Winners will be notified by mail and may be required to complete an affidavit of eligibility and release of liability which must be returned within 14 days of date of notification or alternate winners will be selected. Any guest of a trip winner will also be required to execute a release of liability. Any prize notification letter or any prize returned to a participating sponsor, Bantam Doubleday Dell Publishing Group, Inc., its participating divisions or subsidiaries, or VENTURA ASSOCIATES, INC. as undeliverable will be awarded to an alternate winner. Prizes are not transferable. No multiple prize winners except as may be necessary due to unavailability, in which case a prize of equal or greater value will be awarded. Prizes will be awarded approximately 90 days after the drawing. All taxes, automobile license and registration fees, if applicable, are the sole responsibility of the winners. Entry constitutes permission (except where prohibited) to use winners' names and likenesses for publicity purposes without further or other compensation.

Participation: This sweepstakes is open to residents of the United States and Canada, except for the province of Quebec. This sweepstakes is sponsored by Bantam Doubleday Dell Publishing Group, Inc. (BDD), 666 Fifth Avenue, New York, NY 10103. Versions of this sweepstakes with different graphics will be offered in conjunction with various solicitations or promotions by different subsidiaries and divisions of BDD. Employees and their families of BDD, its division, subsidiaries, advertising agencies, and VENTURA ASSOCIATES, INC., are not eligible.

Canadian residents, in order to win, must first correctly answer a time limited arithmetical skill testing question. Void in Quebec and wherever prohibited or restricted by law. Subject to all federal, state, local and provincial laws and regulations.

Prizes: The following values for prizes are determined by the manufacturers' suggested retail prices or by what these items are currently known to be selling for at the time this offer was published. Approximate retail values include handling and delivery of prizes. Estimated maximum retail value of prizes: 1 Grand Prize ($27,500 if merchandise or $25,000 Cash); 1 First Prize ($3,000); 5 Second Prizes ($400 each); 35 Third Prizes ($100 each); 1,000 Fourth Prizes ($9.00 each) ; 1 Early Bird Prize ($5,000); Total approximate maximum retail value is $50,000. Winners will have the option of selecting any prize offered at level won. Automobile winner must have a valid driver's license at the time the car is awarded. Trips are subject to space and departure availability. Certain black-out dates may apply. Travel must be completed within one year from the time the prize is awarded. Minors must be accompanied by an adult. Prizes won by minors will be awarded in the name of parent or legal guardian.

For a list of Major Prize Winners (available after 7/30/93): send a self-addressed, stamped envelope entirely separate from your entry to: Winners Classic Sweepstakes Winners, P.O. Box 825, Gibbstown, NJ 08027. Requests must be received by 6/1/93. DO NOT SEND ANY OTHER CORRESPONDENCE TO THIS P.O. BOX.

SWP 9/92

The Delaney Dynasty lives on in

The Delaney Christmas Carol

by Kay Hooper, Iris Johansen, & Fayrene Preston

Three of romantic fiction's best-loved authors present the changing face of Christmas spirit—past, present, and future—as they tell the story of three generations of Delaneys in love.

CHRISTMAS PAST by Iris Johansen

From the moment he first laid eyes on her, Kevin Delaney felt a curious attraction for the ragclad Gypsy beauty rummaging through the attic of his ranch at Killara. He didn't believe for a moment her talk of magic mirrors and second-sight, but something about Zara St. Cloud stirred his blood. Now, as Christmas draws near, a touch leads to a kiss and a gift of burning passion.

CHRISTMAS PRESENT by Fayrene Preston

Bria Delaney had been looking for Christmas ornaments in her mother's attic, when she saw him in the mirror for the first time—a stunningly handsome man with sky-blue eyes and red-gold hair. She had almost convinced herself he was only a dream when Kells Braxton arrived at Killara and led them both to a holiday wonderland of sensuous pleasure.

CHRISTMAS FUTURE by Kay Hooper

As the last of the Delaney men, Brett returned to Killara this Christmastime only to find it in the capable hands of his father's young and beautiful widow. Yet the closer he got to Cassie, the more Brett realized that the embers of their old love still burned and that all it would take was a look, a kiss, a caress, to turn their dormant passion into an inferno.